BRECHT
A Practical Handbook

David Zoob

NICK HERN BOOKS
London
www.nickhernbooks.co.uk

A Nick Hern Book

Brecht: A Practical Handbook
first published in Great Britain in 2018 by Nick Hern Books Limited
The Glasshouse, 49a Goldhawk Road, London W12 8QP

Cover image: *The Threepenny Opera*, Royal Academy Opera at Shoreditch Town Hall, 2017; Photography by Robert Workman

Designed and typeset by Nick Hern Books
Printed and bound by Ashford Colour Press, Gosport, Hampshire

A CIP catalogue record for this book is available from the British Library

ISBN 978 1 84842 536 1

For Ana and Kat

Contents

Foreword

David Barnett

Brecht valued a number of qualities in both theoretical and practical work. Clarity, precision and lightness were certainly important, but perhaps the highest praise he could lavish on an idea or an approach was that it was useful. David Zoob's book is eminently useful because it is steeped in years of development and practice. Zoob has engaged with Brecht's many and varied principles for a politicised theatre and channelled them into a wide range of novel and innovative exercises that are applicable to a great many dramas and can equally interrogate devised material.

Zoob's short videos, posted on YouTube, give a concrete flavour of the kind of work you will find in this excellent book. They show how directorial and actorly practice is a collective, collaborative process of discovery. He teases out political aspects that go unspoken or unnoticed in a scene or situation and works through practical solutions. Here he shows how restlessly asking questions and continually seeking answers are the means of creating what Brecht called 'realistic' theatre.

There have been a number of books published recently that take Brecht's theories for the stage seriously and speculate on how they might manifest themselves in the rehearsal room. Zoob's book doesn't speculate; the pages are suffused with the experience of years of practice. This is what makes this book unique: the ideas and exercises are the product of trial and error, reflection and refinement, engagement and achievement. As a result, the reader encounters tried and tested approaches to staging text and dramatic material that are both clear and effective. Zoob presents the reader with a comprehensive array of ideas, methods and exercises that have already shown him and his students their usefulness, and he now passes these on to you.

David Barnett is Professor of Theatre at the University of York. His books include Brecht in Practice: Theatre, Theory and Performance *and* A History of the Berliner Ensemble.

Acknowledgements

I am immensely grateful to Professor David Barnett for his encouragement, rigorous criticism, and insightful suggestions – many of which you will read in the pages that follow; to the stubbornly Stanislavskian Julian Jones for his refusal to let me get away with anything; to Stephen Unwin for his stimulating lectures on Shakespeare and Brecht, and his equally stimulating conversation; to Rose Bruford College for giving me time to start this book; and to Nick Hern whose patience and guidance helped me to finish it. I owe a great deal to the theatre professionals, academic students and actors in training who have debated the ideas and tried the exercises. I must finally thank the family members, friends and colleagues who have had to listen to me rehearsing the arguments and exercises that fill these pages.

*

The author and publisher gratefully acknowledge permission to quote from the following: *The Antigone of Sophocles* by Bertolt Brecht in *Bertolt Brecht, Collected Plays: Eight*, edited by Tom Kuhn and David Constantine; *Brecht on Theatre: The Development of an Aesthetic*, eighth edition edited and translated by John Willett; *Brecht on Theatre*, third edition edited by Marc Silberman, Steve Giles and Tom Kuhn; *The*

Caucasian Chalk Circle by Bertolt Brecht, translated by James and Tania Stern with W. H. Auden; and *Oleanna* by David Mamet, all © Bloomsbury Methuen Drama, an imprint of Bloomsbury Publishing Plc. *Celebration* and *The Lover* by Harold Pinter; *Philistines* by Maxim Gorky, translated by Andrew Upton; and *Stuff Happens* by David Hare, all published and reproduced by permission of Faber and Faber Ltd. *The Cherry Orchard* and *Three Sisters* by Anton Chekhov, translated by Stephen Mulrine, both published and reproduced by permission of Nick Hern Books Ltd. *A Human Interest Story (or The Gory Details and All): A Play for Six Voices* by Carlos Murrilo, published by Dramatists Play Service and reproduced by permission of Carlos Murrilo.

Introduction

'So what's this book of yours about?' I have been asked this question several times by people who don't work in theatre. When they ask this I feel mild panic – I ask myself, why should these people with proper jobs care about the peculiarities of rehearsing plays? But they have asked, so I must answer: I try to describe some of Brecht's ideas in a brief and lively way, and the reply is often the same: 'But that's just good acting, isn't it?' My first instinct is to say: 'No! no! This is a radical challenge to the way things are usually done...' but I stop myself. Their reply is refreshingly encouraging: it suggests that Brecht's theories have more common sense in them than his detractors think. His ideas are often regarded by theatre practitioners as impenetrable and off-putting, to the extent that the theories are fast becoming the preserve of what might be called the 'Theatre Studies Industry'. Worse still, there may be practitioners who have tried to implement the theories and have been confounded by confusions or prejudices among colleagues, and a lack of time to work things out away from the pressures of getting a show on.

Still... if people tell me that actually the theories sound like common sense, then the exercises in this book could offer something of genuine practical use to actors and directors, both in training and in their respective professions.

So why do so many practitioners dismiss Brecht's theories? I would suggest the answer lies in a letter Brecht wrote to an unnamed actor in 1951:

> I have been brought to realise that many of my remarks about theatre are misunderstood.[1]

And why should that be? Bear in mind that 1951 was less than five years before his death, so he is referring to almost *all* of his remarks, although not all were published by then. Anyone who has tried to read *Brecht on Theatre* from cover to cover would agree that his prose is, to say the least, difficult to follow. Moreover, actors frequently complain that 'Brechtian' direction makes them feel like puppets. The unnamed actor above said as much in a letter to Brecht, complaining that Brecht's ideas seem to turn the craft of acting into 'something purely technical and inhuman'. Brecht's reply was that readers would think this because of his 'way of writing'. He then added ruefully 'to hell with my way of writing'.[2]

The result of all this miscommunication seems to be an unhelpful combination of caricature and bafflement. I have seen productions of Brecht's plays cluttered with visual reminders that 'this is theatre and not real life'. These include: props that aren't needed in the scene; huge projected labels scrawled on top of a giant backdrop of sketches representing scenery; an apparatus of 'Brechtian' devices like placards and video projections; cartoon-like characterisations, or characters dressed up to look like the Emcee from *Cabaret*... In the interval, the conversation I overhear most frequently concerns these devices. The uninitiated ask what is the point of all this clutter and they are informed that this is 'alienation'.

This bafflement could well be felt too by the actors, who aren't sure whether they should be performing in a way that's different from 'normal acting'.

The aim of this book is to get past Brecht's peculiar prose and explain the principles of his theories, acknowledging that they changed over time. I have devised short dialogues between an actor and a director in an attempt to represent the frustrations experienced by those actors baffled by 'Brechtian' theory or direction. These are accompanied by a series of practical exercises designed to address the questions these dialogues raise. Should you try the exercises, I encourage you to adapt and develop the techniques *for yourself*: the explanations should clarify the theories, and the exercises are opportunities to test that understanding. Adapt the exercises to suit your needs. It may turn out that the exercises simply help actors to be braver, more physically precise, or more playful.

I hope to demystify the theories and offer an approach to performance applicable to a wide range of texts and theatre styles. These theories certainly can help to bring out the meaning of Brecht's plays, sharpening their impact for an audience. More importantly, they offer an interpretative framework, influencing work on any piece of theatre. They can help us to see and present classic plays differently and are a long way from the 'Brechtian' clichés listed above.

You don't have to agree with Brecht's Marxism to make use of the exercises. Nonetheless, many of the activities in this book have a social dimension: they shift emphasis away from the private, and towards the public; from personal to social, from symptom to possible cause. They are informed by the idea of 'dialectical performance', which means exploiting the provocations that lie in contradictions and juxtapositions. Their impact can be addressed to the emotions as much as to the intellect. They provoke questions rather than providing answers from a political creed or orthodoxy.

There is no specific 'Brechtian' acting style. Performance work influenced by the activities in this book could stylistically resemble a performance resulting from training methods associated with Sanford Meisner or Konstantin Stanislavsky. The difference will be found in the textual interpretation that informs the performances; or, more specifically, the social dynamics that underpin human behaviour.

There is little concern in this book for the notion that being 'Brechtian' requires actors constantly to address or even preach at the audience or 'remind them that they are in a theatre'. People who go to the theatre are perfectly aware of where they are.

Brecht's poems and plays are full of humanity, invention and humour. Turning his theory into practice is rich in those qualities too.

Reading a Text

Astonishment – Interpretation – Strangeness

> Without opinions and intentions one cannot represent anything.
>
> *Bertolt Brecht, 'A Short Organum for the Theatre'*[3]

> It is necessary to rehearse not just how a play should be performed but also whether it should be performed.
>
> *Bertolt Brecht, 'On Determining the Zero Point'*[4]

> If the actors, having acquired a more complete knowledge of the play and a clearer idea of its social purpose, were allowed to rehearse not only their own parts but also those of their fellow actors, the performance as whole could be improved enormously.
>
> *Bertolt Brecht*[5]

Brecht's theatre is founded on the idea that scenes are presented as living illustrations of what he called *Einzelgeschehnisse*,[6] meaning individual events of social significance. A 'Brechtian' reading of any play will involve making these incidents striking and strange, considering their interrelationship, and revealing their social causes.

The reader may be struck by some similarities with some of Stanislavsky's methods in a 'Brechtian' pre-rehearsal textual close reading:

1. Research the play's historical context, considering the possible social-historical factors that influence the characters' behaviour.
2. Break down the text into a sequence of social incidents or events; describe the action of each event. As you do so, consider how odd, outrageous, or astonishing the event might be. In other words, take nothing for granted. Brecht called the list of events produced the *Fabel*, defined as a politically engaged interpretation of the story.
3. Consider each event as a commentary on social conditions and class relations, revealing power dynamics, repression and, where it exists, resistance. The emphasis here is less on a through-line of individual motivation, but instead on the interrelationship of events within the whole narrative. Clashes between or within individuals require *dialectical* interpretation: that is to say, a clash of incompatible forces leading to change within a person, a social situation or wider society.
4. Look for abrupt shifts in action from one event to another, depending on the underlying social cause that is being revealed.
5. As you work through this process, you will arrive at a *Grundgestus* for each extract, i.e. the way a director and ensemble interpret each event within the scene, depicting the nature of the *social relationships* between characters within their *historical context*.

In the two examples that follow, I principally discuss how the scene can be regarded in a preparatory reading. In order to clarify some observations, I stray into the possible ways such readings could be explored in rehearsal practice.

King Lear

Sennet. Enter KING LEAR, CORNWALL, ALBANY, GONERIL, REGAN, CORDELIA, *and Attendants.*

Event 1. Lear announces his intention to abdicate, dividing his kingdom in three parts, passing a third to each of his daughters and their present or future husbands. He requires them to publicly declare their love for him, with the best declaration rewarded with the best portion of the kingdom.

LEAR. Attend the lords of France and Burgundy, Gloucester.

GLOUCESTER. I shall, my liege.

Exeunt GLOUCESTER *and* EDMUND.

LEAR. Meantime we shall express our darker purpose.
Give me the map there. Know that we have divided
In three our kingdom: and 'tis our fast intent
To shake all cares and business from our age;
Conferring them on younger strengths, while we
Unburthen'd crawl toward death. Our son of Cornwall,
And you, our no less loving son of Albany,
We have this hour a constant will to publish
Our daughters' several dowers, that future strife
May be prevented now. The princes, France and Burgundy,
Great rivals in our youngest daughter's love,
Long in our court have made their amorous sojourn,
And here are to be answer'd. Tell me, my daughters,
Since now we will divest us both of rule,
Interest of territory, cares of state,
Which of you shall we say doth love us most?
That we our largest bounty may extend
Where nature doth with merit challenge. Goneril,
Our eldest-born, speak first.

Often this scene is presented as a dignified ceremony, each character seeming to accept Lear's tests as normal and expected, as if the characters had already seen the play or read it beforehand.

A Brechtian reading would make these transactions seem very odd: this means refusing to accept them as fairytale elements designed to set up the story. They are contradictory political acts with far-reaching consequences. Lear wants his private emotional needs to be served by the performance of a public ritual, and this peculiar contradiction illustrates the nature of absolute monarchy.

Rather than quietly accepting the ceremony, all on stage can be ignited by it. Each can be astonished at the strangeness of Lear's initiative. In this extremely public event, every person can carry within them a view on the aged King's rule. Each has aspirations for themselves or others regarding Lear's succession. These energies are further activated when Lear announces the test. As they come to terms with their astonishment, characters can look conspiratorially at potential allies and warily at potential foes.

Event 2. Goneril and Regan flatter successfully. In return Lear grants each a third of the kingdom. Lear points out the boundaries of each third on a map. Cordelia privately rues her inability to flatter.

Continuing from the last note: Goneril and Regan's speeches often come across as rehearsed set-pieces. It would be far more productive for each sister to compose a speech of love on the spot. This 'raises the stakes' for all on stage: their husbands may be tempted to prompt or coach their spouses from the sidelines. In fact, Goneril can think her speech is over with the line 'As much as child e'er loved, or father found' and her spouse may prompt her to add two more lines. If she does this, her words 'A love that makes breath poor, and speech unable' sound like contrived modesty in response to her husband's intervention. The precariousness of the trial of love can be sustained with the ebb and flow of the sisters' confidence and Kent's struggle to hide his dismay at the inappropriateness of the ritual.

GONERIL. Sir, I love you more than words can wield the matter;
Dearer than eye-sight, space, and liberty;
Beyond what can be valued, rich or rare;
No less than life, with grace, health, beauty, honour;
As much as child e'er loved, or father found;
A love that makes breath poor, and speech unable;
Beyond all manner of so much I love you.

CORDELIA. [*Aside*] What shall Cordelia do? Love, and be silent.

LEAR. Of all these bounds, even from this line to this,
With shadowy forests and with champaigns rich'd,
With plenteous rivers and wide-skirted meads,
We make thee lady: to thine and Albany's issue
Be this perpetual. What says our second daughter,
Our dearest Regan, wife to Cornwall? Speak.

REGAN. Sir, I am made
Of the self-same metal that my sister is,
And prize me at her worth. In my true heart
I find she names my very deed of love;
Only she comes too short: that I profess
Myself an enemy to all other joys,
Which the most precious square of sense possesses;
And find I am alone felicitate
In your dear highness' love.

Lear pays for each emotional balm with a large piece of territory. These private, familial exchanges lead to the imposition of new borders on an entire country whose citizens will find themselves living in a new kingdom, now obliged to pledge allegiance to a new ruler. The map can be a large chart placed on a table, held in his hands, or perhaps best of all, placed on the floor. This means Lear can stand on the lands he is about to give away.

These geo-political questions were very much alive when Shakespeare wrote *King Lear* between March 1603 and Christmas 1606. Upon the death of Queen Elizabeth in March 1603, the Kingdom of England came under the rule of the Scottish King James, who spent the early years of his reign attempting to persuade the London Parliament to unite the two kingdoms. The play was performed for King James's Court on 26th December 1606. By this point the King was Shakespeare's paymaster, sponsoring and licensing his company.

This demonstrates that Shakespeare was, to use Brecht's term, *historicising* events, viewing a fictional feudal world through the eyes of the early modern period. The task for the practitioner is to represent the social relations of this feudal world in contrast to those of the present. These resonances won't be lost on a reader in post-Brexit Britain, also aware of the consequences of a possible second referendum on Scottish Independence.

CORDELIA. [*Aside*] Then poor Cordelia!
And yet not so; since, I am sure, my love's
More richer than my tongue.

LEAR. To thee and thine hereditary ever
Remain this ample third of our fair kingdom;
No less in space, validity, and pleasure,
Than that conferr'd on Goneril.

In two essays written in 1940,[7] Brecht proposes that the map should be torn into thirds. This brings the geo-political entity that is England into the room as a significant 'character'. It gives a strong sense of the impact these divisions will have on the land and its people, especially if Lear is standing on a giant map as he tears it. Equally important is Regan and Goneril's attitude to the portions that they receive and the portion that goes to the other sister. Each wants to be sure that they have been rewarded with the best territory (see Chapter Four on *Gestus*).

Event 3. Lear invites Cordelia to play her part in the performance, reminding her that he loves her most and that she is sought after by both the King of France and the Duke of Burgundy. He says he has already earmarked the best portion of land for her. She only has to deliver the most effusive protestation of love to claim it. Cordelia fails to oblige him, and he disowns her in return.

LEAR. Now, our joy,
Although the last, not least; to whose young love
The vines of France and milk of Burgundy
Strive to be interess'd; what can you say to draw
A third more opulent than your sisters? Speak.

CORDELIA. Nothing, my lord.

LEAR. Nothing!

CORDELIA. Nothing.

LEAR. Nothing will come of nothing: speak again.

CORDELIA. Unhappy that I am, I cannot heave
My heart into my mouth: I love your majesty
According to my bond; nor more nor less.

Cordelia attempts to behave in a way that fits with the situation: a public statement of political allegiance is trustworthy if delivered without hyperbole or personal sentiment. For her, hyperbole would be hypocrisy. Lear's response betrays his confusion: he wants sentiment, and he's prepared to reward it with land.

This contradiction frequently features in the corrupt courts of Shakespeare's plays. Hypocrisy is regarded as loyalty, while honesty is a sign of treachery.

Shakespeare's acuity gives us a problem. The plays are so familiar that these contradictions can easily be taken for granted: to paraphrase Brecht, audiences might say, 'Ah Shakespeare! Look at the way he shows how humans are and how they will always be! This is why his plays are so universal, and why this is truly great art!' The task for us is to make this behaviour seem strange, to show *it needn't be like this.*[8] All the exercises in this book are designed to engage with this task.

LEAR. How, how, Cordelia! Mend your speech a little,
Lest it may mar your fortunes.

CORDELIA. Good my lord,
You have begot me, bred me, loved me: I
Return those duties back as are right fit,
Obey you, love you, and most honour you.
Why have my sisters husbands, if they say
They love you all? Haply, when I shall wed,
That lord whose hand must take my plight shall carry
Half my love with him, half my care and duty:
Sure, I shall never marry like my sisters,
To love my father all.

LEAR. But goes thy heart with this?

CORDELIA. Ay, good my lord.

LEAR. So young, and so untender?

CORDELIA. So young, my lord, and true.

LEAR. Let it be so; thy truth, then, be thy dower:
For, by the sacred radiance of the sun,
The mysteries of Hecate, and the night;
By all the operation of the orbs
From whom we do exist, and cease to be;
Here I disclaim all my paternal care,
Propinquity and property of blood,
And as a stranger to my heart and me
Hold thee, from this, for ever. The barbarous Scythian,
Or he that makes his generation messes
To gorge his appetite, shall to my bosom
Be as well neighbour'd, pitied, and relieved,
As thou my sometime daughter.

Lear invokes the gods of his age: these are inviolable symbols of supreme value in his society. Their invocation might make those present kneel or make a show of reverence, but many at Lear's court must feel acutely uncomfortable to do so in support of Cordelia's banishment. This contradiction can be made manifest by the various responses of those present. Some may reveal cowardice and hypocrisy; others may betray reluctance to commit to a ritual that endorses an injustice.

Event 4. Kent attempts to intervene on behalf of Cordelia, while Lear outlines his plan to cede power to his elder daughters while still enjoying the ceremonial status of monarch. He says he will stay with them over alternate months. He passes the crown to them.

KENT. Good my liege –

LEAR. Peace, Kent!
Come not between the dragon and his wrath.
I loved her most, and thought to set my rest
On her kind nursery. Hence, and avoid my sight!
So be my grave my peace, as here I give
Her father's heart from her! Call France; who stirs?
Call Burgundy. Cornwall and Albany,
With my two daughters' dowers digest this third:
Let pride, which she calls plainness, marry her.

As suggested in Brecht's *Buying Brass* dialogues,[9] the enraged Lear can tear Cordelia's portion of the map in half, giving each part to the other sisters. By tearing the map in a state of rage, Lear creates arbitrary borders and portions of unequal size, again illustrating the nature of rule by an absolute monarch. The inequality of this allocation anticipates the strife to come.

I do invest you jointly with my power,
Pre-eminence, and all the large effects
That troop with majesty. Ourself, by monthly course,

With reservation of an hundred knights,
By you to be sustain'd, shall our abode
Make with you by due turns. Only we still retain
The name, and all the additions to a king;
The sway, revenue, execution of the rest,
Beloved sons, be yours: which to confirm,
This coronet part betwixt you. [*Giving the crown.*]

This is a strange, potentially comic moment of contradiction: Lear can divide the land, but not the crown. The elder sisters and their spouses can respond to this in several ways, expressed through the physical precision of a series of '*Not... But*' actions. They could reach for the crown and then withdraw or offer it to the other couple; the others might refuse it when they want to accept. They could all stand powerless, transfixed at a crown that they can't wholly own (see Chapter Four on *Gestus*, in particular the references to objects. There can be few more politically charged objects than a crown).

The above response from the sisters and their husbands, along with the sections of text marked in **bold** below, anticipate the calamities that are to follow. At each moment Lear can notice them and choose to ignore the warnings they carry, indicating that the tragedy arises from human choices rather than the invisible hand of 'fate' (see Chapter Two).

Event 5. Kent resumes his warnings against Lear's folly. The King threatens him with violence, death, banishment and the wrath of pagan gods, none of which can silence the loyal Earl.

KENT. Royal Lear,
Whom I have ever honour'd as my king,
Loved as my father, as my master follow'd,
As my great patron thought on in my prayers, –

LEAR. The bow is bent and drawn, make from the shaft.

KENT. Let it fall rather, though the fork invade
The region of my heart: be Kent unmannerly,
When **Lear is mad**. What wilt thou do, old man?
Think'st thou that duty shall have dread to speak,
When power to flattery bows? To plainness honour's bound,
When majesty stoops to folly. **Reverse thy doom**;
And, in thy best consideration, check
This hideous rashness: answer my life my judgement,
Thy youngest daughter does not love thee least;
Nor are those empty-hearted whose low sound
Reverbs no hollowness.

LEAR. Kent, on thy life, no more.

KENT. My life I never held but as a pawn
To wage against thy enemies; nor fear to lose it,
Thy safety being the motive.

LEAR. Out of my sight!

KENT. **See better, Lear**; and let me still remain
The true blank of thine eye.

LEAR. Now, by Apollo –

KENT. Now, by Apollo, king,
Thou swear'st thy gods in vain.

LEAR. O, vassal! Miscreant!

[*Laying his hand on his sword.*]

ALBANY / CORNWALL. Dear sir, forbear.

KENT. Do:
Kill thy physician, and the fee bestow
Upon thy foul disease. Revoke thy doom;
Or, whilst I can vent clamour from my throat,
I'll tell thee thou dost evil.

LEAR. Hear me, recreant!

Event 6. Lear silences Kent by invoking the feudal order: 'On thine allegiance, hear me!' This succeeds where threats of death and divine retribution had failed. Lear gives Kent ten days to leave the kingdom.

On thine allegiance, hear me!

This moment represents a clash of value-systems. Kent has been attempting to engage Lear's reason, but at the word 'allegiance', rationalist values are brought to heel by those of the prevailing feudal order. The moment can send ripples of energy through the entire ensemble on stage. Kent capitulates and can silently kneel in homage to his feudal overlord; the entire ensemble can follow suit. But should the newly 'crowned' sisters do so? This is another almost comic moment of choice that needs careful choreography to reveal the contradictory consequences of a king wielding absolute power at the moment of his abdication.

Since thou hast sought to make us break our vow,
Which we durst never yet, and with strain'd pride
To come between our sentence and our power,
Which nor our nature nor our place can bear,
Our potency made good, take thy reward.
Five days we do allot thee, for provision
To shield thee from diseases of the world;
And on the sixth to turn thy hated back
Upon our kingdom: if, on the tenth day following,
Thy banish'd trunk be found in our dominions,
The moment is thy death. Away! By Jupiter,
This shall not be revoked.

KENT. Fare thee well, King: sith thus thou wilt appear,
Freedom lives hence, and banishment is here.

To CORDELIA.

The gods to their dear shelter take thee, maid,
That justly think'st, and hast most rightly said!

To REGAN *and* GONERIL.

And your large speeches may your deeds approve,
That good effects may spring from words of love.
Thus Kent, O princes, bids you all adieu;
He'll shape his old course in a country new.

Exit.

Conclusion

The scene presents the contradictions and destructive power of arbitrary and absolute rule in a feudal society. It shows avoidable choices made by a ruling elite that will have terrible consequences for a nation and its people.

The extract represents the interpretative potential of some key theories. The point is not to create a particular acting 'style', but instead to articulate underlying political dynamics and their impact on human action. The examples should demonstrate that, far from turning theatre practice into pamphleteering, employing a 'dialectical' way of seeing can animate and enrich a textual interpretation, showing humans as complex, contradictory and susceptible to change. You could be excused for asking how all of the above insights can be realised in practice. I have offered some practical suggestions, but the following chapters should help directors and performers to find their own ways to meet this challenge, while also finding dialectical insights of their own.

Contradiction

2

> In order to establish society's laws of motion, [materialist dialectic] treats situations as processes and seeks out their contradictory nature. It regards everything as existing only in so far as it changes, or in other words is in disunity with itself.
>
> There is a great deal to human beings... so a great deal can be made out of them. They do not have to stay the way they are; they may be looked at... as they might be.
>
> *Bertolt Brecht, 'A Short Organum for the Theatre'*[10]

The first of the above quotes might appear forbidding: its awkward phrasing is typical of many of Brecht's published theories, and this has contributed to the scepticism felt towards him by some practitioners. Here, he challenges the concept of universal human nature, questioning the idea that a character must be 'consistent'. Consequently he often uses the term 'figure' rather than 'character': the former suggesting something open or incomplete, the latter implying a fixed personality. By examining a figure's actions in relation to the social conditions around them, the actor can reveal both the figure's complexities *and* those of the events acting on them. Brecht is convinced that if the actor concentrates solely on the figure's psychology (i.e. their 'character'), they might not draw an audience's attention to the social conditions that make that figure what s/he is, and what s/he can be.

The Actor and the Director disagree on what makes a realistic portrayal of Lopakhin when working on Chekhov's Cherry Orchard.

DIRECTOR. See if you can play all of Lopakhin's contradictions in this scene. Look for the inconsistencies.

ACTOR. But I need to keep the character consistent or the audience won't believe it's a real person.

DIRECTOR. I don't really care if it doesn't fit with their idea of a real person. We are trying to demonstrate a different realism from the kind the audience is used to.

ACTOR. Oh come on. That sounds so arrogant and pretentious! And in any case, if you are asking me to do things that don't feel consistent with my character, I'll just produce an empty impression. It will have no centre, no soul... no authenticity.

DIRECTOR. Right, so you want all the behaviour in your performance joined together so your character feels to the audience like a 'real person'.

ACTOR. Of course. That's my job.

DIRECTOR. Get someone to video you for a week, and you will see such vivid inconsistencies that you would dismiss your 'performance' of yourself as something 'with no centre, no authenticity' – or whatever you just said. I know you: you are irritable and unreasonable with your wife, you are charming with someone who might give you a job, you are flirtatious with a waitress, and you are terrifying when you are drunk. You are completely inconsistent. Your personality transforms with the changing pressures and influences around you. Why not do the same with this scene?

ACTOR. This is a play, not real life. Characters in plays have to be consistent or they won't ring true. If a character isn't joined together, we'll lose our audience. It will seem arty and arbitrary to them. In fact, it seems pretty arbitrary to me.

DIRECTOR. Aren't the inconsistencies there in the text?

ACTOR. Yes, of course there are shifts... but he's a normal human being. If you keep demanding extreme contradiction you'll turn down-to-earth characters into psychological oddities, violently shifting in mood from one second to the next.

DIRECTOR. But I don't think you are an oddity, and yet you change all the time.

ACTOR. You were talking about filming me for a whole week! This scene lasts a few minutes.

DIRECTOR. As you say, this is a play, not real life.

ACTOR. But essentially he's a straightforward peasant! Well – former peasant. He's the most down-to-earth person in the play.

There may be actors who would delight in the contradictions the director proposes in this exchange; others might wonder which inconsistencies they should play and *how* they should play them. Even if they accept the idea, they may feel compelled to justify contradictions psychologically, so inconsistencies are smoothed out. This would give the performance the appearance of completeness: an actor trained in the Stanislavskian tradition would probably see this a good thing. But Brecht's view was that this would lead to a complete fusion of actor and character, making it impossible for an audience to see the character in any other way.[11] Moreover, if the portrayal all makes perfect sense to the viewer, why should they judge or question the character's actions?[12]

All of the following exercises require the actor to experiment with physical gestures, shapes or actions *before* establishing an 'inner' connection with their character. By working from externals and by listening to feedback offered by observers, the actor can develop an instinct for creating contradictory inner life.

Exercise 1. Playing Contradictions

Purpose: to play contradictions as changes in behaviour which arise from changes in social conditions.

Extract from The Cherry Orchard *by Anton Chekhov*

The speech below is a climactic moment in Act Three of Chekhov's masterpiece. Lopakhin returns from the auction sale of the cherry orchard estate.

RANEVSKAYA. Who bought it?

LOPAKHIN. I did.

A silence. RANEVSKAYA *is overwhelmed. If it weren't for the table and chair beside her, she would fall down.* VARYA *detaches the keys from her belt, flings them to the floor in the middle of the drawing room, and walks out.*

I bought it! Ladies and gentlemen, please, wait – I've a bit of a thick head, I can't speak… (*Laughs.*) When we got to the auction, Deriganov was already there. Leonid Andreyich had only fifteen thousand, and straight away Deriganov bid another thirty, on top of the mortgage. Well, I could see how things were going, so I waded in with forty thousand. He went up to forty-five, so I bid fifty-five. He would go up by five, you see, and I'd bid another ten. Well, it finished eventually. I bid ninety thousand roubles over and above the mortgage, and it was knocked down to me. The cherry orchard's mine now. All mine! (*Laughs.*) Tell me I'm drunk, or crazy, tell me I'm imagining all this… (*Stamps his feet.*) No, don't laugh at me! If only my father and grandfather could rise up out of their graves, and see all that's happened – how their little Yermolai, their abused, semi-literate Yermolai, who used to run around barefoot in winter – how that same Yermolai has bought this estate, the most beautiful spot on earth. Yes, I've bought the land on which my father and grandfather were slaves, where they weren't even allowed into the kitchen. I must be asleep, it's all just a dream, it's all in the mind… It's your imagination at work, shrouded in mystery…[13]

1. Read the speech through out loud, enacting the stage directions.
2. The speech can be seen as an expression of Lopakhin's personal excitement; in Stanislavskian terms, the character's *objective* could be to gain Ranevskaya's forgiveness, and the *obstacle* to this could be the character's own thrill at what he has done. These are Lopakhin's private concerns. By contrast, a 'Brechtian' approach is to consider the speech as a moment in history, in which the old order gives way to the new, anticipating the colossal ruptures to be experienced in that country in 1905 and 1917. Engagement with this task can begin if you mark everything in the speech that exists *outside* Lopakhin, such as the orchard, the observing guests, the memory of the auction or of Lopakhin as a child.
3. Now look at the version printed overleaf. The sections given in bold represent 'points of concentration' chosen to bring out the social and historical nature of the event. If the actor focuses their attention on to these changes, they can transform Lopakhin from moment to moment.

Working with another actor or a director, speak Lopakhin's text while your partner or director reads out the sections in bold. The partner/director should allow the actor time to absorb these sections, following the shifts in attention and physicality. Don't move on to the next section until you feel that you have been changed by the shift described by your partner.

4. Now read both sections yourself, putting the bold sections into the third person. For example 'you notice the guests watching you' becomes 'he notices the guests watching him'. Turning these sections into third-person narrative reminds the performer that they are *showing* another character's behaviour. It also helps to make the actions deliberate and precise.

   Allow each change in the point of concentration to shift where you direct your attention. Each change should act as an imaginative stimulus that affects the way each moment is played.

5. Try the speech again *without* reading the bold sections aloud – simply allowing each one to change you.

RANEVSKAYA. Who bought it?

LOPAKHIN. I did.

A silence. RANEVSKAYA *is overwhelmed. If it weren't for the table and chair beside her, she would fall down.* VARYA *detaches the keys from her belt, flings them to the floor in the middle of the drawing-room, and walks out.*

As Lopakhin, you see the vast expanse of cherry trees in bloom in front of you. An orchard the size of Hyde Park. Your gaze follows the trees into the distance. This is now your kingdom. You are now its conqueror. It gives you vertigo.

I bought it!

Now you notice the guests watching you. They are gentry and bourgeoisie. You are a yokel.

Ladies and gentlemen, please, wait –

They are walking out. They are disgusted by you. You are a dirty, vulgar peasant. You laugh, embarrassed at the momentary humiliation.

I've a bit of a thick head, I can't speak… (*Laughs.*)

They have stopped. These respectable people want you to account for yourself. You feel like a peasant called up before a magistrate…

When we got to the auction,

Remember you are now their conqueror…

Deriganov was already there.

You see the auction room in front of you, placing Deriganov and the others in the space around you. You are now the driven businessman with money in your pocket and dreams of fortunes to be made. Allow this to change your breathing, your posture, the level of tension in your muscles.

Leonid Andreyich had only fifteen thousand, and straight away Deriganov bid another thirty, on top of the mortgage. Well, I could see how things were going, so I waded in with forty thousand. He went up to forty-five, so I bid fifty-five. He would go up by five, you see, and I'd bid another ten. Well, it finished eventually. I bid ninety thousand roubles over and above the mortgage, and it was knocked down to me.

You see the title deed placed before you for your signature. You remember how could you scarcely hold the pen in your shaking hands.

The cherry orchard's mine now. All mine! (*Laughs.*)

You notice his audience again: now you can face them as a man of means.

Tell me I'm drunk, or crazy, tell me I'm imagining all this...

You try to wake yourself from this delirium and find yourself dancing a peasant dance. Perhaps the band starts to play a gypsy tune.

(*Stamps his feet.*) No, don't laugh at me!

They are laughing at the peasant dancing in a landowner's ballroom. How dare they laugh at you! You're the master now!

If only my father and grandfather could rise up out of their graves, and see all that's happened –

You see a serf child standing in front of you, observe his condition, astonished.

how their little Yermolai, their abused, semi-literate Yermolai, who used to run around barefoot in winter – how that same Yermolai has bought this estate, the most beautiful spot on earth. Yes, I've bought the land on which my father and grandfather were slaves, where they weren't even allowed into the kitchen.

You look in an imaginary mirror: you see a rapacious predator. It is horrifying and exhilarating.

I must be asleep, it's all just a dream, it's all in the mind... It's your imagination at work, shrouded in mystery...

This is an example of discontinuity of characterisation, revealing insights into an event of great significance. The speech isn't just about how Lopakhin *feels*: while that's an important part of it, the extract also encapsulates the collapse of an entire social order. To reveal this, we see an individual embodying a multitude of selves, shifting from conqueror to serf to ambitious entrepreneur, reflecting the surrounding social upheaval. The actor frequently focuses on objects outside of himself, referring to memories and identities from past and future, while responding to class reactions in the present. The presentation of this contradictory set of selves should shed light on the tumultuous event acting on them. Note too how the juxtaposition of Lyubov Ranevskaya's reactions to Lopakhin's speech sharpens the contradictions in this event in history.

Some observations from the Actor and the Director.

ACTOR. I can play that, but I'll need to find it gradually as I work my way into the character.

DIRECTOR. Well, yes. Brecht advocated a process in three stages – a, looking at the part with astonishment, finding all that is strange about it; b, allowing yourself to 'enter' the role as you would in a more familiar rehearsal process; c, standing outside the role again, playing the contradictions with greater clarity by bringing to bear the insights gained from b. My concern is that you won't move past b if you strive to justify everything psychologically.

ACTOR. But the changes you have shown me are psychological.

DIRECTOR. Not entirely: they are prompts to your imagination and don't easily conform to the idea of a psychological 'through-line': his thoughts jump all over the place. So don't try to 'motivate' them. You'll make them look too natural.

ACTOR. If I don't motivate the changes, the character will look false.

DIRECTOR. Maybe, but if it looks 'unnatural', that's fine. The point here is to show how humans are never fixed: their behaviour changes with each shift in the conditions acting on them.

ACTOR. That sounds like psychological motivation. You just rejected that!

DIRECTOR. Okay: psychology can be a way of getting there, but I don't think it will give us the definition I'm after. The point of departure here is Lopakhin's *social* position and the way it shifts with the changing conditions around him. So can you find ways of *heightening* the contrast between the changes…? This will show the possibility for humans to change – particularly in crisis moments like this one. It can make an audience feel less empathy and more surprise, and in the process you will show them a world beyond the personal realm of Lopakhin's feelings.

ACTOR. I think I get the theory, but I really don't know how I am supposed to achieve it in practice.

Below is a series of exercises designed to address the actor's last comment on the difficulty of putting theories on contradiction into practice.

Exercise 2. Sharpening the Contradictions

Purpose: to enable an actor to play sharply defined contradictions within a single speech; to draw attention to the social conditions that surround an event.

1. Working again on the Lopakhin speech, deliver *just the commentary* given in bold as a piece of narrative text. Demonstrate the physical manifestation of each change with as expansive a gesture or movement as possible. Ensure that your gaze is directed to a specific place – as demanded by the directions. Differentiate clearly between moments when your attention is on yourself and when on something outside of yourself.
2. Work on it again, allowing physical changes to influence vocal changes.
3. Once you have the changes clearly defined, play them fast without thinking about 'motivating' the shifts.

4. Remove the commentary: you are now playing the speech as a series of movements and gestures. Work on this several times, increasing the speed of the changes while maintaining physical precision.
5. Insert the text, still working with pace and lightness. If you pause, it must be for a good reason. Think of a pause as a measure of the historical significance of what you have just said or done. A line of colossal significance is like dropping a boulder into a small lake, and might need a moment afterwards for its ripples to disperse.

Exercise 3. Making the Unnatural Come Naturally

Purpose: to train in discovering and playing contradictions.

Exercise 2 was a lengthy and challenging process. It may work against many actors' instincts. The following training exercise develops an instinct for this approach and can be used with virtually any text.

Fill a room with chairs, spacing them about three feet apart, facing in all directions. The chairs represent gradations of a particular attitude: if one end of the room stands for a particular extreme, such as happiness or optimism, the other end would stand for misery or despair. Each chair in between is part of the gradation in the spectrum from one extreme to the other.

The chair-spectrum can represent the principal contradiction in a scene or speech: that between financial pragmatism and romantic feeling (see Grusha and Simon in *The Caucasian Chalk Circle*); between courage and cowardice (Mother Courage, Galileo, Azdak in *The Caucasian Chalk Circle*); between lust and repulsion (Proctor in his scenes with Abigail in *The Crucible*); between social confidence and submissiveness (see Lopakhin, above); between ruthlessness and compassion (Mauler in *Saint Joan of the Stockyards*).

1. Change chairs with each shift in thought. Only speak your lines when sitting in a chair.
2. Allow the chair to completely change your breath, rhythm and physical shape.
3. With each repetition of the exercise, increase the distance between the chairs you choose to sit in, maximising the contrasts.
4. Work with an observer or other members of the ensemble. They can draw your attention to the sharpness of your physical definitions and the meanings that arise from the contradictions.
5. Use the chairs to express non-verbally the contradictions in your responses when other figures are speaking.

Exercise 4. Playing the Contradictions

Extract from Philistines *by Maxim Gorky*

Vassilly, a petit bourgeois entrepreneur, is regarded by the other characters as a brute and a bully. The following speech is full of contradictions: he feels compelled to attack his children, but he needs them to love him or he won't feel complete. He speaks cruelly about his daughter, but this comes from love and care for her future. He wants to be proud of his son. He bullies his family but is hurt when his children challenge him. His financial and social positions seem strong, but he's in constant terror of approaching revolutionary upheavals in the streets. He sees securing a future for both his children as a way of protecting himself from his rivals and the simmering revolutionary energies in the streets outside.

VASSILLY. Education? Is a bollocks is all I can see.

Neither of you tell me. Neither of you say what you're thinking. Neither of you give me a hug any more. Neither of you say, 'Good morning, Dad, how are you?' You scowl at me and skulk away like I'm a stranger in the house, ruining your fun. And that hurts. Look at Tanya, withering, a scowling old maid. That's an embarrassment amongst my friends, did you think of that? I don't say she was the greatest beauty in the world, but I can provide a dowry. I would have thought the man lucky to be welcomed into this family. I've seen girls as plain get well married and that's without the sort of dowry I have to offer. And I wanted you to be a lawyer, Pyotr: a member of the town council, an esteemed citizen. A man, Pyotr, proud of his father and a man I could be proud of. Filip Nazarov's son. *Finished* his study, got married, took a dowry, earns upwards of two thousand a year. Already. Filip Nazarov's son, more than two thousand a year. He'll be on the council by the time he's thirty, mark my words. Filip Nazarov, who's just... Filip Nazarov... I mean. He's a bore and second rate. His son. Well, he must be... That's a happy family. That's another hurt.[14]

1. Experiment with gestures of love, entreaty and vulnerability that contrast with Vassilly's strident language.
2. Find ways to physically express his bewilderment at education and at the way his children treat him.
3. When and how does he touch his children? Look for caring gestures of affection as well as those of frustration and anger.
4. Play against his more aggressive language by focusing on his vulnerability or love for his children.
5. Look for moments when his focus is on the streets outside. Find ways of expressing his fear of the future.
6. Place Nazarov and his son in the room. Note how astonished Vassilly is that men of such mediocrity as Nazarov and his son can be on the council.
7. Play the above changes fast, in keeping with the energy of a driven man.

This approach reveals contradictions within Vassilly arising from the crises in his family and those outside his window. They are expressed through sharply defined changes and by playing dissonances between physical gestures and the words.

These contradictions can be developed by using Brecht's '*Not... But...*' technique in which important actions are performed so as to imply that something different could have happened, for example: 'The actor playing Vassilly did *not* embrace his daughter *but* instead scowled and turned away.' By showing the character choosing *not* to do something, and instead doing something else, the actor shows human actions arising from a choice, implying that the character could have done the opposite. This leads to the question: '*Why* did s/he choose that particular action?'

Exercise 5. Fixing the '*Not... But...*'

Purpose: to help the actor reveal contradiction in moments of choice.

1. Look at the *Philistines* extract again, revisiting those moments of vulnerability, e.g. when Vassilly might have had an impulse to show affection or be conciliatory towards his children.
2. Play each of these impulses to the hilt, for example: consider embracing or reaching out to his daughter at any time before the line: 'Look at Tanya.'
3. Replay the scene, playing the impulses again, this time stopping before they are completed.
4. With other members of the ensemble, discuss the reasons why he may have reversed his choice.

   These might be:

   - Something reminds him of his children's ingratitude after he has spent so much on their education.

- Something reminds him his daughter is becoming an old maid, which will make her a financial burden.
- He is distracted by a noise outside, reminding him of the threat from the outside world.

5. Play the scene again, looking for ways to express these insights with physical clarity. Other members of the ensemble should observe and comment on how the choices of physical action read.

Exercise 6. Contradiction: Fixing the '*Not... But...*'

Purpose: to play a choice and reveal the conditions that gave rise to it.

Drama is full of fateful decisions, and the '*Not... But...*' technique encourages an audience to consider them. If a morally questionable action can be shown as arising from brutal social conditions, then the implication is that the choice might be different if the conditions were changed for the better.

Scenario: a child sits on the floor eating some sweets from a bag. An adult walks past, sees the sweets and takes them. The child cries.

1. Play the above scenario with clarity and simplicity.
2. Play it again indicating a moment of choice, for example: the adult could stop after seeing the sweets and contemplate the theft; they could stop before they get to the child; or after they have passed.
3. Each one of these moments of decision can be played as a silent 'aside' to the audience, in which the dilemma is shared; alternatively, it can be played more internally.
4. After the theft, does the adult look back at the child? If the adult looks back with guilt or regret, this can increase the sense that the opposite could have happened.

5. Now establish a social reality in which the action takes place. Perhaps the adult is a starving tramp and the child is privileged; perhaps both are hungry, living in times of great suffering. The more particular your choice of context, the more specific will be your playing of the decision.
6. Look at the relationship *between* events: a noise, a smell, a reminder of hunger, or an action by the child – any one of these could trigger the adult's choice to steal the sweets.
7. Discuss with observers the relative merits of employing explicit non-verbal asides, as opposed to less direct and more implicit communication.

This exercise can train actors to fix the '*Not... But...*' with precision in a variety of contexts. The actor will find greater nuance, depth and complexity by responding to feedback from the observing performers.

Exercise 7. '*Not... But...*' Training

The above examples should introduce the dialectical way of seeing that informs this approach. Regular use of the exercises below, or variations on them, will put this way of seeing into the actor's body, making it part of an habitual performance vocabulary.

'*Not... But...*' Training Exercise A

Someone is selling you an item of clothing from a bonded child labour factory.

1. *Just do it* Buy the item, playing your actions simply. An audience won't be able to say that you have made a conscious choice; nor can they see that you could have done the opposite.

2. *Explore the dilemma* You are about to buy the item when a person with you tells you where it came from. Explore the thoughts that run through your mind and how they make you feel. (This is a version of a 'push and pull' acting exercise often associated with Stanislavsky, which concentrates on the *internal* dilemma of the character.)

3. *Hesitate and decide* Play the scenario again, and as soon as you hear of the item's provenance, stop and think. Explore physically the thoughts in stage 2 to show that the final choice was a *consciously made decision*. Observers note changes in rhythm, gaze, breathing, gesture. Work on these elements to maximise clarity. This will be helped if you show the audience the event as something that happened in the past.

   Note: there is a difference between stages 2 and 3. In 2, the focus is on the internal difficulties experienced by the character in the scenario; in 3, the attention is on showing an audience that a conscious choice was made, and why.

4. *Accept* Buy the item, but with an awareness of the moral compromise. How does this change your rhythms and the way you handle the object? Do you look to see if anyone is watching? Do you turn back after the transaction is complete? If so, why and how?

5. *Refuse* You don't buy the item. Why? Do you regret the choice? Are you full of smug self-congratulations? How is this manifest as you refuse and leave the shop?

As in 3, 4 and 5 place emphasis on showing a choice. In addition, the point is to show that the opposite choice of action is present in the eventual choice: the actor shows what they didn't do as well as what they did.

'Not... But...' Training Exercise B

A neighbour asks a fellow householder on the Kent coast to share the burden of sheltering a large family of Syrian refugees.

1. *Discuss the scenario* Establish clear given circumstances and a simple sequence of events. Work out why the neighbour might refuse. It could be that they distrust refugees, or are fearful of what the community will say, or think the action might be illegal.
2. *Play the scenario. You refuse the request* Show why you refused through physical actions: this might involve looking suspiciously at the refugees or looking warily to see if you are being watched. It might be that you look at the size and make-up of the family and fail to see how you could fit them into your house.
3. *Repeat the scenario. You accept* Incorporate the actions in 2, but this time you grant the request.
4. *Refine the work* Observers can comment and give detailed advice on the physical actions required to reveal, firstly, that the opposite could have happened, and secondly, *why* the character chose the way they did.

Conclusion

Contradiction and the *'Not... But...'* have numerous applications. Brecht's plays are full of financial transactions, and the technique can reveal their human as well as financial cost. In *Mother Courage and Her Children* there are occasions when Courage can choose *not* to repudiate her way of living; in *Macbeth* there are moments when Macbeth chooses *not* to act on an impulse to reject his wife's exhortations; in *Three Sisters,* Andrei decides *not* to challenge his wife; in *Death of a Salesman,* Happy Loman decides *not* to publicly admit that the deranged man in the restaurant is his own father. In each case the performer can consider whether they want to show the viewer *why* the decision was made, or whether they want them to work it out for themselves.

Working on ways to play inconsistencies can also equip the actor to work on material traditionally regarded as antithetical to Brecht. Howard Barker's characters speak and feel in violent non sequiturs; Ionesco's tragic marionettes have such short memories that their moods change like the 'oddities' the actor refers to above. These writers reject social causality, but more importantly they reject *psychological* justification for the instability of their characters. The actor simply has to surrender to the demands of the text, and the exercises in this chapter can help to liberate actors from inhibition. '*Silence*' is a frequent stage direction in *Waiting for Godot*: each time it appears, actors could replace it with 'They do not speak', indicating that silence is a choice, provoking performers and spectators to consider why this choice is made. In the final lines of that play, Vladimir and Estragon could be about to move after they say: 'Shall we go? / Yes, let's go.' They could then *reject* that option, giving the ending added poignancy: these tramps now have an understanding of their situation, but the tragedy is that it's no use to them.

Practitioners today are uncomfortable with seeing Shakespeare's Shylock as a medieval villain. Contradiction is a useful way of humanising him: indeed, he needs to make himself swear 'an oath to Heaven' to maintain his demand of a pound of flesh from Antonio. There are moments in the trial scene when he could contemplate sparing his victim; an audience could observe him forcing himself to keep his bond *with regret*, as if he wishes it were otherwise; they could see a man chained to a burdensome obligation to god. (In Brecht's poem 'The Mask of Evil', he exclaims: 'What a strain it is to be evil.') There are several contradictions in the scene before Shylock dines with the gentiles. Here he tells his daughter to lock herself up in his house and repeats how he is loath to leave her. He can be seen on the one hand as vengeful miser, a villain, and the comic archetype of a Possessive Father; but on the other as a loving, caring, single parent, a victim of constant cruelty, frightened to enter the world of gentile persecution. He must dine with the gentiles to seal the bond and so gain his revenge: but he can hardly force himself to go.

You may legitimately observe that if every moment of choice is revealed in the ways I suggest above, it would turn a two-hour play into a four-hour epic. Selectivity is called for, and in the next chapter, I will discuss how taking on the role of storyteller can give a performer a narrative grip on an entire episode, giving a framework for such judgements to be made.

Storytelling

> Everything hangs on the 'story'; it is at the heart of the theatrical performance. For it is what happens between people that provides them with all the material that they can discuss, criticise, alter.
>
> The actor masters his character by first mastering the 'story'. It is only after walking all round the entire episode that he can, as it were by a single leap... seize his character.
>
> *Bertolt Brecht, 'A Short Organum for the Theatre'*[15]

'Just tell the story' is a note that directors frequently give to actors. By this they probably mean: 'Don't get so involved in your own character that you forget what the scene is about.' They might not always say that's what they mean, and nor do they always say how the actors can achieve that. This chapter will attempt to explain what Brecht meant by 'story' and how his interest in 'narrative' over 'plot' can illuminate meaning. It will discuss the changes in mental perspective and physical action that the performer needs to make in order to elucidate narrative meaning for an audience.

A storyteller narrates in the past tense, and Brecht is saying that he wants actors to perform as if they are showing events that have already happened. Most plays require actors to perform events as if they are taking place in the present, so Brecht's approach may seem counter-intuitive. His purpose is to shed a particular light on events, explaining, analysing, and criticising human activity. This process offers new perspectives on familiar events, making the spectator less inclined to accept them as inevitable. He argued that placing events in the past made it easier to see the political and social mechanisms underlying the characters' actions.

The convention of playing 'in the past tense' facilitates almost every other aspect of Brecht's approach to making theatre. It enables actors to 'stand apart' from the characters they are playing, and implicitly comment on what they did. It often requires physical definition of the characters' social positions through selective use of movement, gesture and space. It draws attention to the choices characters make and allows audiences see why they were specific to particular circumstances, rather than 'universal' representations of 'human nature'. The exercises that follow will touch on these concepts and approaches, which will be developed in later chapters.

Actors, in the Stanislavskian tradition, usually make choices arising from their character's 'objectives', and these are in turn determined by 'given circumstances'. While this may still be the case for a actor performing 'in the past tense', the emphasis shifts from the needs of a character to the needs of the story as a whole. It's as if the play – or indeed the playwright – is a character with particular objectives, and the actor is performing them on their behalf. In these exercises, the actor is encouraged to identify these objectives and to subordinate the needs of their character to them.

Narration frames action in a way similar to the caption in a billboard advertisement; it sets up expectations before an event or comments on the action after it. Action can reveal what narration doesn't tell an audience, and vice versa. In plays that feature a narrator, this interplay between narration and action is a vital means by which a play's meaning is articulated. These exercises are designed to give the actor tools that exploit this relationship. By sensitising the actor to the ways narrative can be constructed, this work is indirectly applicable to plays that don't feature direct-address narration.

The Actor and the Director disagree over different ways of making theatre.

DIRECTOR. Play this scene as if the action has already happened. There's no need to convince an audience that it's all actually happening *now.*

ACTOR. But the scene *is* happening *now.* It's not like there's someone on stage reading from a story book...

DIRECTOR. I said 'as if'. *As if* you are showing past events. It's about a state of mind, I suppose.

ACTOR. But how do I get into this 'state of mind'? And in any case, why put the scene into the past when it's not *written* in the past tense?

DIRECTOR. It's a bit like the action replay or expert analysis at half-time or after a football match. I actually feel physically sick when I watch England play. I am so terrified and excited that I feel nothing but anxiety and disgust for all our players. I scream at them, desperate to make them play better, I yell at referees when they make decisions against us, and if England actually score I collapse into ecstasy. My judgement is, well, *clouded.* But at half-time, when the action is replayed and analysed, the experts can show, from a variety of angles and perspectives, what has been going on in terms of tactics and disputed decisions. Storytelling theatre gives the performer the vocabulary to offer this kind of insight.

ACTOR. But we don't do that in the theatre. The scene is shown just once. There are no replays.

DIRECTOR. True, but events can be shown from a variety of perspectives, and storytelling gives you the means to do that.

ACTOR. You haven't explained how.

DIRECTOR. To perform in this kind of work you will need to place your attention on the story and not on yourself.

ACTOR. But my attention isn't on *myself*: it's on what my character wants and on what happens around me as I play those wants.

DIRECTOR. Yes, that's fine, but it's one approach – and not the only one.

ACTOR. It has worked perfectly well for hundreds of years: actors playing intentions and the audience grasping the overall meaning by taking in the story as a whole.

DIRECTOR. Yes, but that approach risks overwhelming everything with suspense and emotional immediacy – so much so that something really important could pass them by.

ACTOR. Theatre works *because* there is suspense and immediacy and emotion. Why restrain the very energies that make theatre powerful? And why insist on spelling everything out as if we are performing to an audience of children?

DIRECTOR. I don't think it's about spelling things out: it's about articulating events clearly. We aren't telling them what to think – but we *can* show them something they didn't expect. They can be astonished if we shed new light on events.

ACTOR. Such as...?

DIRECTOR. X is a businesswoman. Her business fails, her husband leaves her and X curses her double-dose of bad luck. Y is a rival businesswoman: her business succeeds, she gets rich and claims credit for the outcome. If the story is told in a way that just focuses on the characters' private travails, the audience would say: 'Oh how typical of X's gold-digger spouse to abandon her...' Or: 'How typical of human nature to blame fate when things go wrong, and take the credit when they go well.'

ACTOR. They might say any manner of things! It depends on how they see the play and how it's written. And anyway, who are we to decide how they should respond?

DIRECTOR. My point is that if we show the story as a series of historical events, pointing at possible causes, we can encourage an audience to question whether the behaviour really was 'typical' and whether the events really were inevitable. We can help them gain a clearer understanding of the values and mechanisms that led to the unfortunate outcome.

ACTOR. That sounds extremely didactic and propagandist.

DIRECTOR. I think we can agree we both want to avoid that...

ACTOR. But Brecht's focus on coldly explaining and questioning seems to get in the way of passion, spontaneity and humanity.

DIRECTOR. I see no reason why we can't still achieve that with this approach...

Storytelling and 'Theatre-Making'

The work of a storyteller-actor blurs the distinction between actor and director, and even between actor and writer. These exercises are designed to give a performer an instinct for this type of work, enabling them to shape narrative events so that the performance articulates an agreed interpretation. This approach equipped members of Brecht's Berliner Ensemble to make vital contributions to productions. A famous example is Helene Weigel's 'Silent Scream' at the sound of the firing-squad volley that killed one of her sons: this memorable moment in the production of *Mother Courage and Her Children* was neither written in stage directions nor given as direction from Brecht himself. It was created by an actor utterly in tune with the aims of the play and production. Like many moments from Brecht's own productions, it is a powerful riposte to the Actor's criticism that this approach lacks passion and humanity.

Exercise 8. Aesop's Fable of the Eagle and the Fox

Purpose: to enable the performer to discover ways of marshalling narrative by exploring the relationship of storytelling to action and the sequencing of events.

The Fable

An Eagle and a Fox had become close friends and decided to live near each other. The Eagle built her nest in the branches of a tall tree, while the Fox crept into the undergrowth and there produced her cubs. Soon after they had established their new homes, the Eagle discovered she had nothing with which to feed herself and her young. Overwhelmed with hunger and fear for her offspring, she waited until the Fox was away from her cubs, and swooped down into the Fox's den. She seized one of the little cubs, on which she and her young feasted. The Fox, on her return, discovered what had happened, and was enraged. The Eagle flew off in search of new prey. She was hovering near an altar, on which some villagers were sacrificing a goat, swooped down and grasped a piece of the flesh in her talons and flew off back to her nest, unaware that a burning cinder was stuck in the flesh. It wasn't long before a strong breeze ignited the coal, and the helpless eaglets were roasted in their nest. Their charred bodies dropped down dead at the foot of the tree, where the Fox devoured them.

The exercise is intended for groups of three within a larger workshop group. Each trio comprises one narrator and two actors.

1. The group discusses the 'moral' of the story.

This is a simple fable demonstrating that when amoral selfishness becomes the norm, suffering will ultimately return to plague the perpetrator. In a particularly cruel way, the events make the Eagle experience what it feels like to suffer the very agonies she had inflicted on her neighbour. The story implicitly proposes a world in which we treat others as we would wish to be treated by them.

2. The group agrees the key events that make up the story.

There are probably nine. They can write these down as an agreed narrative skeleton. They discuss which of these events is a climactic moment in the story.

3. The group decides on style.

The performers can decide the extent to which they represent the animals literally. One approach is to apply techniques derived from animal study to produce an accurate human imitation of the animal. Alternatively, they can find a human *equivalent* to the animals. Either way, the aim is to represent the intentions and actions of each character with clarity and simplicity, bearing in mind the agreed point of the story.

4. The storyteller narrates and the performers enact what they hear.

5. The performers lead the storytelling.

In stage 4 above, performers are simply illustrating the narrator's description of events, so information is being given twice. Now, in certain sections, the narrator can experiment with remaining silent, allowing the performers to enact the events.

6. The narrator offers commentary.

The group discusses which sections worked best when enacted without narration, and why. They enact them again, and this time the narrator can look for ways to add something to what has been shown. For example, a performer playing the Eagle may represent the raptor's dramatic swoop on her prey, clutching the hapless cub in her 'talons'. The cub yelps in terror and pain and the narrator comments: 'The Eagle was hungry: her young needed to be fed.' The comment is a clear provocation to the audience and relates to the 'moral' of the fable; it is not description, but ironic juxtaposition.

7. The group decides on sequencing.

The performers discuss whether narrative/comment should come before or after the action in this and other juxtapositions in the story.

8. The group tests the material.

The group tries out their options and choices in 5 and 6 above, asking an audience of fellow practitioners what meanings they took from the various options.

9. The group applies these principles to the rest of the story.

The performers choose other events in the story and explore the possibilities offered by juxtaposing action with narrative/ commentary.

In the exchange at the beginning of this chapter, the Actor observes that most plays aren't written this way: despite this, a performer can apply the principles of this exercise to any scene, particularly those from Brecht's plays. The better an actor understands how a scene is structured, the more effectively they will convey its story. The deeper their understanding of the impact of a particular way of sequencing events, the more sensitive they will be to the interrelationship of events in the scene. The stronger the actor's grasp of how juxtapositions communicate meaning, the greater the impact will be on the way they present the juxtapositions of words and pictures in the scenes.

Exercise 9. The Eyewitness to a Shooting

Purpose: to experience 'showing' rather than 'being' a character.

This is based on Brecht's 'Street Scene' exercise.[16] It shows how a re-enactment of an event requires an actor to 'stand outside' his/her part; it also shows how precise demonstration can enable the viewer to form an opinion on the events.

An incident in North Charleston, South Carolina, USA, following a traffic stop

At 9.30 a.m. on 4 April 2015, Mr X, a fifty-year-old forklift driver, was driving a 1991 Mercedes and was pulled over by a police officer on Remount Road, Charleston, North Carolina, for having a broken brake light. He was on his way to an auto-parts store when he was stopped. Mr X was aware of a court warrant demanding he pay child support at that time.

Officer Y, aged thirty-three, pulled him over and spoke to him. As the policeman returned to his car, Mr X got out of his car and fled, with the policeman running after him. He chased him into a lot on 5634 Rivers Avenue, where there was an argument between the men. Officer Y fired his Taser, hitting Mr X, who fled again. The policeman stopped, planted his foot, drew his weapon and aimed it at him, firing eight rounds at Mr X's back. When Officer Y fired, Mr X was approximately five metres from him and running away. The coroner's report stated that he was hit three times in the back, once in the buttocks and once on one of his ears. Officer Y radioed in: 'Shots fired. Subject is down. He grabbed my Taser.'

The police officer didn't realise he was being filmed by a passer-by. The video showed that that there was no danger to the policeman. The video showed the officer walk up to Mr X's prostrate body and turn around, dropping the Taser by the body before he walked away.

Officer Y claimed Mr X fought him and tried to take his Taser. He didn't deny shooting him in the back. A witness said: 'Mr X never tried to grab the Taser. He was just a regular guy. Fifty years old, drove a forklift truck. He wasn't a gang member. He didn't look like a gang member. He just looked like a scared ordinary guy, running away.'

A toxicology report showed that Mr X had cocaine and alcohol in his system at the time. The cocaine level was less than half the amount for 'typical impaired drivers'. Mr X's police record listed ten arrests: for contempt of court regarding failure to pay child support or to appear for court hearings; he was arrested in 1987 on an assault and battery charge and convicted in 1991 for possession of a cosh.[17]

In this exercise, devise a presentation made by two eyewitnesses working together.

1. Decide on the moments that need to be shown. Mark them in the script.
2. Read the report aloud, physically representing each of the moments you have chosen. Each moment is a short event, rather than a picture: you are showing to a third party what happened, not making tableaux. Actions and gestures must be precise, distances as exact as possible. Dialogue can either be quoted or a version of what the report implied was said.

3. Consider how the presentation would alter if you were showing it to: a) the press; b) a legal inquiry; c) a group of activists. Experiment with these changes of audience.
4. In what ways is the audience's perception changed by the information in the toxicology report and background information on Mr X?

This exercise demonstrates the seriousness of Brecht's endeavour. In his theatre, humans are the objects of a socially important inquiry, often with real lives at stake.

Exercise 10. The Prelude to Brecht's *Antigone*

Purpose: to identify and play the physical realisation of pivotal moments in the narrative.

This incorporates many of the conventions explored in the above exercises. An important difference is that one of the sisters is both narrator and 'actor'. The dialogue is in the present tense, but the framing narrative indicates that it is action that took place in the past.

1. Read the Prelude aloud as a group.

Berlin. April 1945.

Daybreak.
Two sisters come back to their home from the air-raid shelter.

FIRST SISTER.
And when we came up from the air-raid shelter
And the house was whole and in a brighter
Light than dawn from the fire opposite
It was my sister who first noticed it.

SECOND SISTER.
Sister, why is our door open wide?

FIRST SISTER.
The draught of the fire has hit it from outside.

SECOND SISTER.
Sister, what made the tracks there in the dust?

FIRST SISTER.
Nothing but someone who went up there fast.

SECOND SISTER.
Sister, the sack in the corner there, what's that?

FIRST SISTER.
Better that something's there than something's not.

SECOND SISTER.
A joint of bacon, sister, and a loaf of bread.

FIRST SISTER.
That's not a thing to make me feel afraid.

SECOND SISTER.
Sister, who's been here?

FIRST SISTER.
How should I know that?
Someone who's treated us to something good to eat.

SECOND SISTER.
But I know! We of little faith! Oh luck
Is on us, sister. Our brother is back.

FIRST SISTER.
Then we embraced each other and were cheerful
For our brother was in the war, and he was well.
And we cut and ate of the bacon and the bread
That he had brought us to feed us in our need.

SECOND SISTER.
Take more for yourself. The factory's killing you.

FIRST SISTER.
No you.

SECOND SISTER.
It's easier on me. Cut deeper.

FIRST SISTER.
No.

SECOND SISTER.
How could he come?

FIRST SISTER.
With his unit.

SECOND SISTER.
Now
Where is he, do you think?

FIRST SISTER.
Where they are fighting.

SECOND SISTER.
Oh.

FIRST SISTER.
But there was no noise of fighting to be heard.

SECOND SISTER.
I shouldn't have asked.

FIRST SISTER.
I didn't want you scared.
And as we sat there saying nothing a sound came
In through the door that froze the bloodstream.

A screaming from outside.

SECOND SISTER.
Sister, there's someone screaming. Let's see who.

FIRST SISTER.
Sit still. You go and see, you get seen too.
So we did not go outside the door
To see what things were happening out there.
But we ate no more either and we did not
Look at each other again but we stood up and got
Ready to go to work as we did daily
And my sister took the plates and I bethought me
And took our brother's sack to the cupboard

Where his old things are stored.
And I felt, so it seemed, my heartbeat stop:
In there his army coat was hanging up.
Sister, he isn't in the fight
He's run for it, he's cleared out
His war's over, he has quit.

SECOND SISTER.
Those still there, he's left them to it.

FIRST SISTER.
They had death lined up for him.

SECOND SISTER.
But he disappointed them.

FIRST SISTER.
There was still an inch or two…

SECOND SISTER.
That was where he crawled through.

FIRST SISTER.
Some still in, he's left them to it.

SECOND SISTER.
His war's over, he has quit.

FIRST SISTER.
And we laughed and we were cheerful:
Our brother was out of the war and he was well.
And as we stood there such a sound came
It felt like ice in the bloodstream.

A screaming from outside.

SECOND SISTER.
Sister, who is it screaming outside our door?

FIRST SISTER.
Again they are tormenting folk for pleasure.

SECOND SISTER.
Sister, should we not go and find out who?

FIRST SISTER.
Stay in. You go and find out, you get found out too.
So we waited a while and did not go and see
What the things that were happening outside might be.
Then we had to leave for work and I was the one who saw
What it was outside our door.
Sister, sister don't go out.
Our brother is home but he is not
Safe and sound but hanging there
From a meat hook. But my sister
Went out of the door
And screamed herself at what she saw.

SECOND SISTER.
They have hanged him, sister. That was
Why he cried out loud for us.
Give me the knife, give it here
And I'll cut him down so he won't hang there
And I will carry his body in
And rub him back to life again.

FIRST SISTER.
Sister, leave the knife.
You'll not bring him back to life.
If they see us standing by him
We'll get what he got from them.

SECOND SISTER.
Let me go. I didn't while
They were hanging him. Now I will.

FIRST SISTER.
And as she made for the door
An SS man stood there.

Enter an SS MAN.

We do not know the man.

SS MAN. We know who he is. Say who you are.
He came out of here.

Seems to me very probable
You know that traitor to his people.

FIRST SISTER.
Sir, we are not the ones to question.
We do not know the man.

SS MAN.
So what's she doing with the knife, her there?

FIRST SISTER.
Then I looked at my sister.
Should she on pain of death go now
And free our brother who
May be dead or no?[18]

2. In groups of three, identify the 'nodal points' or moments around which the action hinges, i.e. moments that change the course of the action, for example:

- Point 1 is probably the moment when the second sister asks why the door is open, since this discovery leads them into the house. Without it they may have stayed in the street outside.
- Point 2 is probably: 'Sister, the sack in the corner there, what's that?'

  It leads them to…
- Point 3: 'A joint of bacon, sister, and a loaf of bread.'

  Leads to…
- Point 4: 'Oh luck / Is on us, sister. Our brother is back.'

In each case the second sister is making these discoveries, so she is clearly moving forward throughout, with the other sister behind.

3. Once you have gone through the scene establishing each nodal point, work out what you want to reveal about these characters and how to enable an audience to clearly see what is significant – like the action replay referred to in the Actor–Director argument.

Consider each sister's physical characteristics. These features need to be carefully selected to reveal how each sister has been shaped by war: one is clearly cautious, the other is impulsive. One has taken on the responsibilities of the elder sister, the other exhibits contrasting characteristics.

4. Create a staged picture of each nodal point.

Avoid making lifeless tableaux. In other words, make sure actions are motivated and can be followed through. In some cases you could attempt to play the action twenty seconds before and after the nodal point, so as to ensure it is alive. (You won't always be able to do this if the nodal points follow each other quickly.)

Throughout this exercise the third person in the group can observe and comment. You can rotate this role.

5. Consider the timing of events.

So, in the section with the line: 'Sit still. You go and see, you get seen too', you need to work out when the sister sits and how. Sister 2 can go back to her chair after: 'Sit still', or after: 'You go and see, you get seen too'. If you choose the former option, you will show that Sister 2 automatically submits to her sister's authority. If you choose the latter option, you will show that Sister 2 decides to sit down so as not to be seen outside. Which meaning best serves the point of the story?

Exercise 11. Events and Objects

Purpose: to identify nodal points, so the storyteller focuses on events.

Sometimes an event is represented as the entrance of a character or the focus on a significant object, like a cinematic close-up on an object of dramatic importance. These exercises require an actor to find a theatrical equivalent.

Drawing Attention to Important Objects

Purpose: to create a relationship to imagined or real objects, conveying their narrative function and what they reveal about the characters.

1. All of the objects in the scene below from the play *A Human Interest Story* by Carlos Murillo are imagined by the speaking characters. Draw a plan of the living room, working out where the objects are. Place them in positions that will help you to show the audience around.

2. Now walk through the imaginary space and furniture, using the text to enable the spectator to see each object and gain a sense of its significance.

PAULA. It's eleven o'clock –
and if you are very quiet
and step carefully through the snow so as not to make crunching sounds with your boots
you can move here to the window.
And once by the window,
you can press your nose up to the frosted glass,
look through the window
and see what's happening inside.

KELLY. Shhhhh…

PAULA. You'll see a living room.
A living room of a young, married couple
that could be anywhere in America

KELLY. that voted Democrat in the last election.

PAULA. A television.
A couch that folds out into a bed.
An antique roll-top desk –
inherited from a grandmother –
cluttered with bills, bank statements and other neglected correspondence.
Framed posters of art-museum exhibitions.
On a side table
A Tiffany lamp

KELLY. (wedding gift from an old high-school chum)

PAULA. and magazines –
Vanity Fair, *Vogue*, *The New Yorker*, *Wallpaper*.
A CD collection –
organised alphabetically and by genre –
expectedly eclectic –
classic rock, jazz, soul, European electronica, blues
and most well-represented in the collection,
music from the genre known as –
for lack of a more specific word –

KELLY. 'alternative music' .

PAULA. A few film and Broadway-musical soundtracks.

KELLY. No speed metal.

PAULA. No gangsta rap.

KELLY. Against the wall you'll see a bookcase
lined with titles covering a variety of subjects and genres –
indicative that the couple who live in the house enjoy reading,
are not experts in any particular given subject,

PAULA. but know a little bit about a lot of things,

KELLY. making them welcome conversationalists at dinner parties and other social gatherings.[19]

Drawing Attention to Events

Purpose: to find ways of drawing the viewer's attention to the most important events in a story.

You will have noticed that this work usually requires an actor to make physical choices and play them in what may be regarded as a 'demonstrative' style. This contrasts with Declan Donnellan's view as expressed in his excellent book *The Actor and the Target*, which is that the actor should avoid showing anything.[20] By this he means that, once the actor has engaged imaginatively with objectives, the external manifestation of the character's intentions should take care of itself. A storytelling approach frequently requires the performer to do the reverse: play the external manifestation with clarity and the 'inner life' should take care of itself.

The two speaking characters here are not really characters at all. The writer asks each company that stages the show to give them the names of the actors who play them.

The hierarchy of events

The 'external manifestation' here comes from playing stresses implied by the text.

The most important dramatic events are in bold type.

Find a way of delivering the text so as to highlight their importance. Also, the writer has arranged the layout of the text to help this, with rhythms determined by the length of each line.

Context

Paula's husband has read her diary and discovered her infidelity. Recently she had lost a child when pregnant. Reading the diary makes him realise the child wasn't his.

PAULA. Press your nose against the frosted glass and you'll see:
The front door opening.

KELLY. Wow… look at her…
That's his wife.
Watch her as she enters the house through the front door.
She wears a red winter overcoat
She carries a sack of groceries

PAULA. (she asked for plastic AND paper)

KELLY. **and a leather briefcase.**

PAULA. She stomps the snow stuck to her boots on a green mat by the door.
She puts down the briefcase and bag of groceries on a small table,
removes her coat
and hangs it on a peg on the wall.
She's about to enter the living room
but freezes when she sees
Her husband.
…
She tries to muster up words, something to say
But thirty-six hours of silence has made words near impossible.

KELLY. The front door is behind the couch so he has his back to her,
making it easier for him to meet her entrance with silence.
Making it easier not to acknowledge her.

PAULA. She watches, perfectly still.
She notices the sofa bed, open.
She notices the six bottles of Sam Adams on the side table. Empty.
She notices,
Sitting on the sofa bed in front of her husband,
Her green velour diary.
Open.
Her mouth opens slightly as if to say something.

KELLY. As if his shoulders can sense this,
as if wanting to silence her
he raises the bottle of Samuel Adams to his lips
and takes a long sip.

PAULA. She bows her head and tightens her lips.

KELLY. He stares straight ahead and tightens his lips.
The woman does not move.

PAULA. **The man does not move.**

- Use these textual features to deliver the objective of conveying the most important events to the audience.
- In a 'laboratory' workshop, experiment with the direction of your gaze in a selected section. When do you look at the imaginary objects and when do you look at the audience? Use the feedback you receive from your audience to make decisions on this that you can apply to the rest of the extract.

Exercise 12. The Storyteller and Power-shifts in a Scene

Purpose: to identify the power-shifts in a scene, and ensure they are played clearly.

Extract from The Lover *by Harold Pinter*

Unlike the previous extract, the following are texts written in the more familiar present tense. These are rehearsal exercises to help the actor identify important details in a scene. They are also useful for those occasions on which a director feels that the performer's articulation of these details is unclear.

The Lover is set in an English suburb in the 1960s. A respectable couple appear to have an open relationship in which Richard nonchalantly accepts the frequent visits of Sarah's male lover, Max. The action reveals that this lover is in fact a fictional character played by Richard himself. Their life is represented as a series of role-play scenes, in which Richard either plays the lover or the husband. In each one, Richard inserts unexpected questions or 'facts' into the role-play, threatening its stability, and ultimately its existence. This extract takes place during one of Max's visits. The couple are now drinking tea having just made love under a table in the living room.

- Once you have read through the following (ideally, of course, you should read the whole play), insert a sentence *before* each line that explains how much power your character has at that moment, and how that is shown by what the character does.
- Deliver the inserted line directly to someone who is watching the scene. Do so before delivering your line from the play. Every detail in your narrative insertion should be manifest in the way you play the subsequent moments. If an observer can't see it, keep working on the line until it's apparent.

- I have given possible insertions for the opening section. I would encourage you to decide on your own. Having just done this for the first seven lines, I noticed how the exercise ensures that a detailed and specific acting choice is made for each moment.
- When playing the narrative inserts, you may feel that you are standing outside your character. This is another way of expressing Brecht's idea that the actor 'shows' and comments on their character when performing it.
- Actors may feel this is an excessively painstaking or even painful exercise, robbing the scene of its electricity and spontaneity. So once you have worked through the text in this way, you can remove the insertions while attempting to retain the specificity they facilitated. The idea is to complement the precision of past-tense narration with present-tense spontaneity.
- You may need to balance this exercise with subsequent work exploring the chemistry and tension between the characters.

First, here's the scene without commentary.

MAX *sitting on a chair downstage-left.*

SARAH *pouring tea.*

SARAH. Max.

MAX. What?

SARAH (*fondly*). Darling.

Slight pause.

What is it? You're very thoughtful.

MAX. No.

SARAH. You are. I know it.

Pause.

MAX. Where's your husband?

Pause.

SARAH. My husband? You know where he is.

MAX. Where?

SARAH. He's at work.

MAX. Poor fellow. Working away, all day.

Pause.

I wonder what he's like.

SARAH (*chuckling*). Oh, Max.

MAX. I wonder if we'd get on. I wonder if we'd... you know... hit it off.

SARAH. I shouldn't think so.

MAX. Why not?

SARAH. You've got very little in common.

MAX. Have we? He's certainly very accommodating. I mean, he knows perfectly well about these afternoons of ours, doesn't he?

SARAH. Of course.

MAX. He's known for years.

Slight pause.

Why does he put up with it?

SARAH. Why are you suddenly talking about him? I mean what's the point of it? It isn't a subject you normally elaborate on.

MAX. Why does he put up with it?

SARAH. Oh, shut up.

MAX. I asked you a question.

Pause.

SARAH. He doesn't mind.

MAX. Doesn't he?

Slight pause.

Well, I'm beginning to mind.

Pause.

SARAH. What did you say.

MAX. I'm beginning to mind.[21]

I will now give suggested commentary for two sections from this extract. The commentary is inserted before each line, since it should be delivered as narrative before you speak the line in the original text.

Section 1

MAX *sitting on a chair downstage-left.*

SARAH *pouring tea.*

SARAH. **She stopped pouring tea. Unsettled by his thoughtful stillness, she addressed him.**

Max.

MAX. **He sat still, preparing to ask about her husband. He answered absently, presenting himself to her as preoccupied with what he is about to do.**

What?

SARAH. **She felt weaker so she tried to get his attention affectionately, by saying:**

(*Fondly.*) Darling.

MAX. **He increased his power by remaining silent and motionless.**

Slight pause.

SARAH. **She covered her loss of power by replying seductively:**

What is it? You're very thoughtful.

MAX. **He maintained his power by replying firmly and remaining still and silent.**

No.

SARAH. **She moved closer to him with playful seduction to make him speak, as she insisted:**

You are. I know it.

Pause.

MAX. **He refused to succumb by remaining still, his gaze fixed on the opposite wall. He then asked quietly:**

Or:

He increased the pressure on her by turning and looking her in the eye, asking:

Where's your husband?

Section 2

MAX. **He intensified his hold on her by leaning towards her, his face nearly touching hers as he asked:**

Why does he put up with it?

SARAH. **She stood her ground and confronted him, maintaining eye contact and demanding:**

Why are you suddenly talking about him? I mean what's the point of it? It isn't a subject you normally elaborate on.

MAX. **He stood his ground, repeating the question in a voice that was too loud with his face so close to hers:**

Why does he put up with it?

SARAH. **She attempted to hide her defeat by turning away:**

Oh, shut up.

MAX. **He stood up and stated coldly:**

I asked you a question.

Pause.

SARAH. **She turned back to face him breathing slowly to retain her composure, then replied defiantly:**

Or:

She turned back to face him, and to regain control, playfully brushed his hand with hers, replying seductively:

He doesn't mind.

MAX. **He turned away, asking nonchalantly:**

Doesn't he?

Now I encourage you to insert your own commentary for the entire extract. It should contain a reference to the power dynamic and to its verbal and physical manifestation in the way the line that follows is delivered. It is perfectly possible that you won't use any of these choices in the final outcome, but the exercise should give precision to all your textual and physical choices. Brecht would see this exercise as a means of articulating power mechanisms in class relations: here the power relations are about gender, each character conforming to the gender roles typical of their time and place.

Exercise 13. The Storyteller and Social Hierarchy

Purpose: to draw attention to the relationship between social position and behaviour.

The exercise can alert the actor to actions in which power and social position are in unexpected tension. It encourages the actor to consider how a person of habitually little influence will behave when they find themselves with power.

Extract from Oleanna *by David Mamet*

In this play, a student has lodged a complaint against her professor on the grounds that his teaching methods and language are offensive and threatening. In this section from Act Two, he has called her into his office to persuade her to withdraw the complaint. In the first act, she felt intimidated and her behaviour was timid. She has since gained advice from a support group. The extract below begins with the final section of a speech in which Carol condemns John's behaviour.

Insert a comment before you speak that reminds your audience of your social position before describing the character's action in the past tense, and its level of influence. I have given a few suggestions – the rest are up to you. You can insert the student's non-verbal responses to the professor's long speech as well as commentary on his actions in the speech itself.

CAROL. **The student used her newfound eloquence to express her outrage at the way the professor had treated her. She delivered her condemnation before standing up to leave.**

I tell you. That you are vile. And that you are exploitative. And if you possess one ounce of that inner honesty you describe in your book, you can look in yourself and see those things that I see. And you can find revulsion equal to my own. Good day. (*She prepares to leave the room.*)

JOHN. **The professor had a flash of inspiration about how to make the student see things differently. He stood up, calling to her:**

Wait a second, will you, just one moment.

The professor noticed that the student had stopped, but not turned back. He tried to regain his composure, and said evenly:

(*Pause.*) Nice day today.

CAROL. **The student was baffled and annoyed that he had undermined her. She turned and demanded:**

What?

JOHN. **The professor felt like a teacher again, in command of his subject.**

You said 'Good day.' I think that it is a nice day today.

CAROL. **The student knew it was not a nice day, so she was irritated with the professor for playing another trick.**

Is it?

JOHN. **The professor could see that he had stopped her from leaving by intriguing her. He pressed home his advantage.**

Yes, I think it is.

CAROL. **The student was exasperated by the professor's self-satisfaction, but she was interested enough to ask:**

And why is that important?[22]

Exercise 14. The Provocative Storyteller

Purpose: to use narrative to provoke an audience to make decisions.

Plenty of plays articulate political positions, and the above techniques will help to articulate them in all their complexity. But it is probably a bad idea to think of a play as having a 'message': if that's all a playwright can manage, s/he might as well write the message down and pass it round before the show. It's more productive to think in terms of the provocations that the play offers its viewers. This exercise will help you find ways of *standing outside* your character to encourage an audience to judge them. It can be used in any scene in which characters act in morally contentious ways.

A useful extract for this example is Scene Ten of *Stuff Happens* by David Hare (you will need to read the entire play beforehand). In this scene, Tony Blair and George W. Bush stroll through the grounds of Prairie Ranch, Crawford, Texas, discussing Bush's plans for invasions in the Middle East.

In the section that immediately follows, an actor can play Blair and simultaneously take the role of a barrister, first defending and then prosecuting him. Simply insert a comment before those lines of Blair's that represent key pieces of evidence, for example: as defence counsel you might insert comments like this:

> BLAIR BARRISTER. **My client's motive was to save the Middle East from an abominable tyrant, and to protect the United Kingdom from the threat of Weapons of Mass Destruction. He wanted evidence that would legitimise the actions that would arise from this entirely legitimate motive. We can see this when he said:**

> BLAIR. I've been thinking. I've had this idea. I need – I don't know – tell me if you think this is crazy, David – I think it might help if we had some sort of *dossier*. A kind of *dossier*.

> MANNING. What kind of dossier?

BLAIR BARRISTER. **My client wanted evidence that would stand up under International Law. He wanted a UN resolution. He reasonably assumed his intelligence services would have this evidence, which is why he said to Manning:**

BLAIR. I'd have thought, I don't know, surely the intelligence services can put something together?

MANNING. You mean, from sources?

BLAIR BARRISTER. **My client wanted the evidence to be made public. We can see that he knew he had to be straight with the British electorate when he said:**

BLAIR. Just the facts. Spelt out – very simply, very clearly, about the dangers of Iraq developing and using their weapons of mass destruction.

As prosecution, you might insert the following:

PROSECUTOR. **The defendant's motive was self-aggrandisement. Look at the way he talks – it's all about him. 'I need' he says. He wanted evidence cooked up to justify a war plan that was already decided on. Look at the egotism, the manipulation, and the dishonesty when he said:**

BLAIR. I've been thinking. I've had this idea. I need – I don't know – tell me if you think this is crazy, David – I think it might help if we had some sort of *dossier*. A kind of *dossier*.

MANNING. What kind of dossier?

PROSECUTOR. **We can see that the defendant invented Saddam's crime and then demanded the evidence to 'prove it' when he said:**

BLAIR. I'd have thought, I don't know, surely the intelligence services can put something together?

MANNING. You mean, from sources?

PROSECUTOR. **We see that the defendant talked of facts, but they were about the danger of Iraq having weapons, not proof that they had them, when he said:**

BLAIR. Just the facts. Spelt out – very simply, very clearly, about the dangers of Iraq developing and using their weapons of mass destruction.[23]

It's important that I don't influence your decisions, so I'll stop there. If you are prosecuting, elsewhere in the extract you might insert something like: 'Look at the way the accused was only interested in maintaining his position as Prime Minister when he said – ' Or, 'Look at the way he wilfully misunderstood Richard Dearlove's judgement on the intelligence, saying – '

Your barrister's standpoint should influence the way you play Blair's lines. Find details in movement, gaze, rhythm and textual emphasis that illustrate the barrister's position. (This is an example of *Gestic* acting, and I will develop this further in Chapter Four.) This should enable you to provoke your audience to condemn or exonerate the former Prime Minister. They must reach a decision. Sharing moments of astonishment will remind an audience that no action by those in power should be left unquestioned and no moral outrage should be taken for granted.

Now play the scene *without* the barrister's comments, but with the presence of a courtroom in your imagination. Allow everything you do to be determined by your overall objective, which is to make the court either exonerate or condemn your character. Now that you can't verbally articulate your commentary, it can become active in the way you present your character's actions and respond to those of others. Everything you do is with an awareness of an audience of jurors who have to reach a verdict. They are part of the performance, so you can look at them and communicate with them both with text and non-verbally.

Exercise 15. Storytelling a Moment in History

Purpose: to draw attention to the social causes of events and predicaments; to question their permanence and inevitability.

Brecht called this *historicisation.* He wanted each event to exhibit all that was particular and distinctive about its historical period. This was to remind an audience of their transitory nature and remind us that our era is also impermanent. By emphasising a scene's historical context, we can view the past from the perspective of the present, seeing that values, attitudes or suffering are not for all time, but are specific to their time and place, and subject to change.

In Act Three of Chekhov's *Three Sisters*, Olga suggests that Irina should marry the unprepossessing Baron Tuzenbach. Here is the extract, with numbers indicating each event:

1. Irina gives expression to her despair, mourning her loss of youth and hope. She questions the value of her existence.

> IRINA (*trying to control herself*). Oh, I'm just so miserable… I can't work, I won't work, I've had enough of it! First I worked in the telegraph office, now I have a job with the town council, and I despise everything they give me to do… I'm twenty-four already, I've been working for ages, my brain's dried up, I've become thin, and old, and ugly – there's no satisfaction in any of it, absolutely none, and time's passing, and I feel as if I'm moving further and further away from a genuine, beautiful life, and heading into some kind of abyss. I'm in despair, I don't know why I'm still alive, why I haven't killed myself before now. I don't understand it…

2. Olga says Irina's crying is upsetting her, so Irina stops and tells Olga to notice this.

> OLGA. Don't cry, darling, don't cry… It hurts me…

> IRINA. I won't, I won't cry… Enough… Look, I've stopped crying… It's over…

3. Olga suggests Irina should marry the Baron. Irina cries again.

OLGA. Oh, my dear, I'm speaking to you now as a sister, as a friend… If you want my advice, you should marry the Baron.

IRINA *quietly weeps.*

4. Olga justifies her suggestion and gives her views on marriage.

After all, you respect him, you think highly of him… True, he's not good-looking, but he's a decent man, clean-living… I mean, women don't marry for love, they do it out of duty. At least, that's what I think, and I'd marry without love. I'd marry anyone that asked me, as long as he was a decent person. I'd even marry an old man…

5. Irina condemns her past dreams as nonsense.

IRINA. I kept waiting, waiting for us to move to Moscow, and I'd meet my true love there. I've dreamt about him, loved him… But it's turned out to be nonsense, all of it…

6. Olga embraces Irina, repeats that the Baron is so ugly that it made her weep and then repeats her instruction that Irina should marry him.

OLGA (*hugs her sister*). Oh, my dear, darling sister, I understand everything. When the Baron left the service, and came to see us in his civilian clothes, he looked so awful that I actually started to cry… And he asked me, 'Why are you crying?' What could I tell him? But if it's God's will that he should marry you, I'd be very happy. That'd be quite different.[24]

If the actors focus on wants, needs and feelings, the scene could be trapped by its emotional power, with the result that it comes across as an incurable calamity. Historicising the action can point to the causes of her predicament, reminding us that she is trapped by her class, by the backwardness of her surroundings and by Russia's failure to enter the era of economic and social modernity. Viewing an historical period through the lens of the present can encourage the actor playing Irina to consider her character's potential to resist her 'fate'.

a. Before they speak, the actors insert a line of narration that refers to their character's social position. They speak of their character in the third person, for example:

   OLGA. **The General's eldest daughter expressed her sympathy for her distressed younger sister:**

   Oh, my poor darling…

   IRINA. **The General's youngest daughter controlled herself and listed the reasons for her despair:**

   (*Trying to control herself.*) Oh, I'm just so miserable… I can't work, I won't work, I've had enough of it!

b. The actors insert a line directing the viewer's attention to what is socially significant each time their character says something of importance, for example:

   IRINA. **Look at the way Irina, the educated youngest daughter of a Russian general responds to being trapped in a provincial backwater:**

   First I worked in the telegraph office, now I have a job with the town council, and I despise everything they give me to do… I'm twenty-four already, I've been working for ages, my brain's dried up, I've become thin, and old, and ugly – there's no satisfaction in any of it, absolutely none, and time's passing,

c. The actors insert a line that directs the spectator's attention to the way their character reacts to what the other character says, again with focus on social conditions.

For example, before Olga speaks the lines quoted below, Irina's actor can comment as follows:

Look at the way Irina desperately struggles to accept a miserable marriage: her life in a remote town has taught her to do so.

Or:

Look at the way Irina vainly *resists* accepting the lot of a woman of her class living in a remote town.

OLGA. After all, you respect him, you think highly of him… True, he's not good-looking, but he's a decent man, clean-living…

…and another example:

Look at the way Irina was appalled that Olga's description of marriage could apply to her own marital life:

OLGA. I mean, women don't marry for love, they do it out of duty.

Note: This section of the exercise inevitably focuses on Irina's commentary and its physical manifestations. In order to deliver her commentary, the actor playing Irina will have to interrupt Olga's speech repeatedly. It is likely to take several attempts for the actor to find physical shapes and actions that express the commentary most clearly.

Conclusion

Brecht's reference to 'walking around the entire episode'[25] almost sounds like he's describing a piece of immersive theatre. The companies that devise this kind of theatre, as well as those that have come from the Paris movement schools, such as L'École Internationale de Théâtre Jacques Lecoq and L'École Philippe Gaulier, have employed theatre-making techniques akin to this notion of actor-storyteller.

They make theatre with an awareness of the relationship between each component of a production, creating meaning through the interaction of performance, design and sound.

Additionally, the examples in this section indicate the application of this approach to plays written in a 'naturalistic' style, since an emphasis on *showing* can address the difficulties faced by actors who are told their work isn't communicating clearly. Likewise, illuminating the underlying social or political mechanisms in a scene can open up new meanings in any play and can be used in even the most Stanislavskian of rehearsal processes and supposedly naturalistic of texts.

Showing, elucidating, and commenting: these have been the essential features of this approach to theatre-making. They require performers who are well trained in physical precision. As I mentioned earlier, they require *Gestic* acting, which is explored in the next chapter.

Gestus: Part One

Training

4

Brecht's directorial method was based on investigation and varied experimentation that could extend to the smallest gestures – eyes, fingers... Brecht worked like a sculptor on and with the actor.

Hans Curjel on Brecht's 1948 Antigone[26]

Each moment and each gesture was chosen and composed... Everything... was part of the composition.

Lee Strasberg on Brecht's 1956 The Caucasian Chalk Circle[27]

The Actor and the Director are unsure of what Gestus *means.*

ACTOR. You are clearly very interested in using Brecht's ideas, but you never seem to talk about *Gestus.*

DIRECTOR. Talking about theories in rehearsal usually doesn't get us very far.

ACTOR. Do you use *Gestus* in rehearsal?

DIRECTOR. Well... no. I'm never sure if people will understand what I'm talking about. I'm not even sure if I know myself...

ACTOR. I used to think it was another word for gesture.

DIRECTOR. Yes, it involves gestures, but *Gestus* doesn't actually mean 'gesture'. I think it's more a question of selecting gestures or actions to show what's significant.

ACTOR. Which is what actors do anyway.

DIRECTOR. Yes, but selected to elucidate a particular way of seeing or standpoint.

ACTOR. And in Brecht's case, that way of seeing concerns social class. But how is that different from ordinary character work?

DIRECTOR. Maybe it isn't that different: I think this will take a lot of working out, partly because he keeps using the term in different ways. There is always a social dimension and he's keen to stress it's what happens *between* people.

ACTOR. Isn't there also a reference to the staging? The *Gestus* of the blocking?

DIRECTOR. Yes, expressing the *Grundgestus* or basic standpoint of the whole scene, an exchange or an action...

ACTOR. This is really odd: he comes up with a concept that seems to be really important to him, and he can't say definitively what he means by it!

This exchange reflects some of the difficulties arising from the various ways Brecht uses a term that has no simple English translation. This introductory exercise is designed to enable performers to use a *Gestic* approach in a variety of ways.

Exercise 16. Making *Gestic* Choices in Practice

Purpose: to shift the focus from psychological to social, Gestic *choices.*

[A forward slash in the text indicates a point of interruption by the next speaker. A dash on its own indicates that the speaker doesn't know what to say.]

A DOCTOR*'s surgery. The* DOCTOR *is looking through some notes. The* NHS PATIENT *sits in front of the* DOCTOR.

DOCTOR. Yes, we have the results of your endoscopy and… well: they do show a small growth. It is a non-malignant and / so the next –

PATIENT. What does that mean – ?

DOCTOR. It means there is no visible evidence that the cell growth is out of control. It poses no threat to any of the surrounding tissues and there is no apparent danger of it spreading. But we will need to keep an eye on it, and remove it sooner rather than later. So the / next thing to –

PATIENT. So I will have to have surgery…

DOCTOR. Yes… The next stage is for us to set a date for removal. It is a very straightforward procedure. You'll be out in a couple of days.

PATIENT. So I'm not in danger of…

DOCTOR. No. There are no signs of morbidity. So the main thing is to get rid of it, and you need to see my secretary to set a date.

PATIENT. –

DOCTOR. That's… that's all for now. All right?

PATIENT. Thank you.

The PATIENT *leaves.*

If the actor playing the doctor focuses on psychological objectives, it is likely s/he will show a diligent, if perhaps rather impersonal, physician. There is nothing wrong with this, and this chapter isn't an attempt to assert one approach as superior to another. But performers can experience the process of making *Gestic* choices if they start from a simple political intention for the scene.

If the purpose of the scene is to comment on the current state of the NHS, then the way the actor performs will change profoundly. Following are two scenarios among many that we can explore here.

Scenario I: The doctor is under severe time pressure, driving through the consultation to meet consultation targets in an overstretched practice.

- Consider how the doctor sits or stands, the extent of eye content with the patient, the tempo and rhythm of movements, speech and gesture.
- Explore the details of each of the above considerations, discussing with observers how each choice reads to a spectator.
- These choices can become sharper if they are achieved at some cost: the doctor may try to be sensitive, but the drive and stress will compromise this. This should make the portrayal human and not just propagandist. The tension between sensitivity and hurry might produce a powerfully manifest contradiction in the doctor's physical actions and energies.

Scenario 2:This doctor isn't interested in her/his NHS patients, instead prioritising private practice to maximise income.

Given the doctor's interests as defined above, experiment with all the *possible physical manifestations* of the doctor's *attitude* to this patient. As you physically work through the thoughts below, look for the strongest choice to serve the agreed point of the scene.

- If the doctor is standing, where is s/he standing? How is s/he standing? What is s/he looking at?
- Is the doctor sitting? How does s/he sit? Does s/he get up? When does this happen? Does s/he look out of the window; where is the best position for the window? What is s/he looking at? Is it his/her car? Is it the next patient's car? Who is the next patient?
- What is the doctor's rhythm? Is s/he slow and lazy or working fast to get rid of the patient? Is it both? When does it change?
- What activities can the doctor do to indicate why s/he treats this patient in this way? Could s/he be on the phone, or looking at the next patient's file?
- Consider the *timing* of his/her actions: at what point is the doctor most distracted, i.e. when does the patient need the doctor's attention most?
- Explore *the patient's responses*, and at all costs *avoid playing the victim*. What is the patient's reaction to this treatment if the point is to demonstrate Brecht's view that 'nothing should be taken for granted'?[28] In other words, what responses from the patient would prevent an audience from feeling fatalistic ('Yeah, they're all like that. What do you expect?'), and instead provoke a more proactive response?
- A choice of *Gestus* can be deliberately contradictory: *if the doctor offers a handshake at the end*, this contradicts the idea that s/he is trying to expel the patient quickly. It could disarm the patient, whose feelings of outrage will have intensified by this point. A handshake here suggests that the doctor has charmed the patient into accepting the way the consultation went, shedding light on the power relations in the scene. This action also gives the patient a

strong moment of choice: can s/he shake the doctor's hand in such a way as to show that s/he could have done the opposite?

This careful selection of physical manifestations to contribute to social commentary amounts to *Gestic* acting in practice. The example illustrates how it requires actors and directors to *insert* physical shapes or actions that offer social commentary on an exchange. This insertion will usually focus on the public rather than the private or psychological. I have worked on this exercise with university students. When we asked them where the (in this case male) doctor would prefer to be, a student replied 'on the golf course'. I asked them what the actor could do to show this, and the students then proposed that the doctor could – facing the audience – lazily practise his golf swing, just after the patient asks what 'malignant' meant.

Summary: two important features of this approach:

1. The starting point is the 'social significance' of an event, rather than the psychology of the characters. Once the social standpoint is agreed, the actor and director choose actions for the character that will best communicate it.

2. The emphasis is on working with physical externals. Psychological motivation or a psychological 'through-line' is secondary. Actors often refer to this as 'working from the outside in'.

Exercises for Training in *Gestic* Acting

Gestic acting arises from – and draws attention to – a character's social standing, which can only be understood in relation to others.[29] Simultaneously, it comments on it and supports a socially engaged interpretation of a play. It consequently requires a high degree of selectivity and physical precision; performers have to be physically literate and able to craft actions and shapes that offer a *Gestic* commentary. Below is a series of exercises designed to provide the performer with the beginnings of such a vocabulary.

Exercise 17. Status Energies

Purpose: to increase physical articulacy and awareness of physical actions as potential social commentary.

Gestus is a character's basic socially defined physicality. It can then be transformed by a character's changing attitudes to events taking place around them. Brecht called these changes of physical bearing *Haltungen* (plural), frequently using the singular noun, *Haltung*. Here is an exercise designed to sharpen an actor's physical precision and deepen their imaginative engagement with *Haltung*. It is based on a version of what Keith Johnstone calls 'Status':[30] this term doesn't necessarily refer to social standing, although it can relate to it. Rather, it expresses levels of physical assertiveness. In the list below, each 'status' level implies precise *Haltungen*, or physical characteristics. I have also suggested that you experiment with 'opposing impulses' as a way of exploring the tension of contradiction. Impulses that contradict a character's typical status are always a struggle to fulfil.

These exercises can be worked on in a group of up to eighteen. For much of the time the workshop leader can feed in the descriptions and instructions below, and the performers can work solo, responding to imaginary people as the scenarios develop. The workshop leader may also choose moments to put two actors with the same status into a scenario or an exploration of 'opposing impulses'. The exercises often produce comedy and should be fun to do: they illustrate Brecht's assertion that 'a man who is not having fun himself cannot expect anyone to have fun watching him'.[31]

Level 1: Agoraphobic You are locked inside your house, terrified to go out. You occupy a tiny amount of space. Your gaze is to the floor. Your movements might be sudden, slow, or you may be still, but they are motivated by varying levels of terror. The world terrifies you, as do other people. Experiment with an *opposing impulse*. Try to sing out loud, try to dance.

Level 2: Painfully Shy You eventually pluck up the courage to leave your house or flat. Experiment with a tempo and rhythm to your walk as you try not to draw attention to yourself. You want to run this errand as quickly as you can and get back to the safety of your home. Buy something in a shop. How fleeting is your eye contact with the shopkeeper? How do you respond when they ask you to speak up? How do you feel when their hand touches yours as they give you the change? Try and act on an *opposing impulse* such as declaring your love for someone or making a public announcement.

Level 3: Embarrassed You have developed a habit of giggling to cover your embarrassment. The sound of your voice makes you embarrassed, and your embarrassment makes you nervous. You now raise your eyes and make eye contact with people more, but embarrassment kicks in when it lasts too long. You feel better when you try to laugh it off. Go into another shop where the products are piled high; you carefully avoid knocking them over. Well done. You meet someone you know. You are attracted to them. Your embarrassment makes you move suddenly. You knock over the products. Try to pick them up. Say goodbye to the person you met, and apologise to the manager. Oh – you just knocked a carton of milk out of another customer's hands as you were turning to the manager. Again, useful *opposing impulses* might be to declare your love for someone or to make a public announcement.

Level 4: Noisy You have noticed that making people laugh makes you feel better about yourself. So now you try to make jokes all the time. You are the clown in a group of friends. You notice that they don't listen to you very much. Try to get their attention. Tell a joke: they aren't listening so you raise your voice. How do you feel when they tell you to be quiet? What are your physical rhythms and tempo? How do you use your hands? How much space do you take up? *Opposing impulses*: try to give serious instructions about defusing a bomb; teach someone how to operate a chainsaw.

Level 5: Sensible You have noticed that your clowning antics just made you feel like an idiot. So now exercise some self-control. Try to find a quiet dignity in everything you do. Be respectful and often deferential. A waiter in an expensive restaurant will often cultivate this *Gestus*. Your breathing is shallow; try to deepen it. Servants in period dramas become expert in playing this status. Something goes wrong in an aristocratic household: you attempt to disappear, trying – but not always succeeding – to deepen your breathing. Use stillness, alertness, casting wary glances around you. What is the best tempo to enable you to survive? Where is your eye line? Try to hold someone's gaze without seeming impertinent. *Opposing impulses*: try to swear or cheer a football team; attempt to release some 'road rage'.

Level 6: Dull but persistent; sometimes neurotic You have now been promoted to lower or even middle management. You don't have much flair, but you have plenty of stamina. You can go on and on at meetings without noticing that people are struggling to stay awake. You can hold someone's gaze and make presentations, but if you attempt to push yourself beyond your station, you feel the anxiety of 'impostor syndrome'. Make a presentation. Do you notice that your voice has been droning on for a long time? At intervals notice the look of scepticism or boredom in your audience. Do they affect you? If not, soldier on. If they do, how does that feel and what does it make you do? How do you deal with a question you can't answer? A person on this level struggles with self-doubt or even crisis when they feel out of their depth.

Level 7: The Salesperson This is similar to level 4, but with more drive and less idiocy. You might be described as a 'wide boy' or 'wide girl': you live on your wits and can sell anything. Sell an imaginary customer a car or a photocopier. Show them the product's features. Notice your gestures and rhythms as you develop your patter. Dare to let your eye contact linger; you can dare to joke with the client. Are you comfortable touching them or even flirting? Your enthusiasm is forceful to the point of aggression but sometimes you employ level 5's deference – but not for long. It is a small part of your striving to make a sale. *Opposing impulses*: go into a church, apologise for making too much noise; try to show reverence or quiet respect at a funeral.

Level 8: Affable You have developed ease and charm. Your gestures are open and generous. You can assert yourself without being aggressive; you take up space, your head still and your eye-line level. You are friendly, enthusiastic and a good listener. Go to a pub or bar and greet your friends. This sort of status is how many of us would like to appear. Your body is centred, the muscles are relaxed, your breathing steady, your actions and gestures seem effortless. You are a great diplomat because it is difficult to detect any ulterior motives in your actions. *Opposing impulses*: neurotic or obsessive worrying; feelings of extreme jealousy or even rage. Explore the struggle between these impulses and the ease of your 'natural' state. See what happens when neither of the opposing forces wins out.

Level 9: James Bond/Superhero/Supermodel The ease and charm have now become extremely cultivated. You can appear arrogant to some. Your tempo is slower than level 8, and you might be described as 'cool'. As a model you are aware of your beauty and of the presence of a camera, but you hide the fact that you are playing up to it. Experiment with changing your behaviour depending on whether a camera is pointed at you. How are you dressed? What shoes do you wear? How do you handle props?

How do you eat and drink? How do you read the label of an expensive Bordeaux? *Opposing impulses*: feelings of grief, terror, and impulses to do something silly. Try to keep such forces internalised, but present.

Level 10: Human Deity This is an unusual status and one that is rarely seen among real-life mortals. It is found more frequently in myths and Bible stories. There are some ultra-charismatic figures who give off an 'otherworldly' quality. Brecht would doubtless scorn such behaviour as that of con artists, and on some occasions this is a type of *Gestus* conferred upon a person by hysterical admirers. Walk as if your feet don't touch the ground. Your gaze isn't just level, it extends to the horizon, your calmness is unnerving. *Opposing impulses*: try to laugh, to tell a dirty joke.

These status exercises could be used as part of daily training for a company of Brechtian actors. Each status position must never be seen as the natural state of a person: for Brecht, all behaviours are momentary expressions of a socially constructed 'self' and are subject to change. Over time the exercises will help the performers to refine physical choices and find detail in the tensions of opposites. They can also use each *Gestus*/status in particular scenarios. There are examples later in this chapter.

Exercise 18. Shifting *Gestus*

Purpose: to develop awareness of moments of change in Haltung*; to develop physical precision when playing each change.*

If behaviour is a series of momentary responses to given conditions, changing with each alteration in those conditions, then *Gestic* acting requires a performer to make sharply defined physical transformations.

1. The figures.

The performer has to represent three figures:

- The CEO of a company.
- The middle manager.
- A shop-floor worker.

2. Find the physical bearing for each figure.

With the above status exercises in mind, experiment with the typical *Gestus* of each figure. How do you walk, sit, or stand? What is your tempo? How much space do you take up? What are you wearing? What is your most familiar environment and activity?

The above can be developed and refined with the use of observation. You can also use photographs or film footage of useful role models.

All three of the figures have the same text:

> A manufacturer's design fault has been detected on the
> most recent model. We now have to withdraw it from
> the market. That means recalling twenty thousand units.
> All units need to be back with us by the end of the week.

3. Explore the text.

a. The CEO delivers the text to the middle manager, whom s/he blames.

   The CEO turns and delivers the same text to his/her board, who blame him.

b. The middle manager delivers the text to the CEO. First, as if it is the middle manager's fault; secondly, as if it is the CEO's fault.

S/he turns and delivers the text to the shop-floor worker. First, as if s/he blames him; secondly, with the knowledge that it's his/her own fault.

c. The shop-floor worker delivers the text to the middle manager, with no interest in blame.

   The shop-floor worker turns and announces the text to their colleagues on the shop floor, who are on productivity pay.

4. Play each of the above combinations with no words.

Once you have worked on the physical precision for each one, present a chosen pairing to the ensemble wordlessly, keeping the face as neutral as possible. The ensemble can guess which pairing is being delivered. You can use a neutral mask if one is available.

Exercise 19. Defining *Haltung* in a '*Not... But...*'

Purpose: to develop precision when selecting Haltungen *(the plural form of* Haltung*) to articulate the social significance of a scene.*

The actor's choices of physical bearing can comment on a scene. This is an example of how *Gestic* choices can illuminate the social significance of a transaction and the several moments of choice within it.

A is a person wearing a coat. B is a pawnbroker on a market stall.

B, sitting on a chair at a desk, centre, checks a ledger on the desk.

A arrives wearing a coat. Sees B. Stops. B looks up; they make eye contact. B looks back down to the ledger. A walks up to B. B looks up again. A stops, removes the coat, offers it to B.

B takes the coat, inspects it, lays it on the desk. B takes three coins from his/her pocket, counts them, and offers them to A.

A takes the coins and leaves. B puts the coat on the back of the chair and returns to the ledger.

1. Establish the 'social significance' of the scene. It might be:

- That poverty is degrading.
- That exploiting desperate people hurts the exploiter as much as the victim.
- To demonstrate the consequences of a gambling addiction.
- To demonstrate the emotional dynamics of revenge if B once abused A in the past, and this is an opportunity for payback.

Whichever of these you choose, you will arrive at a particular *Fabel* or politically engaged interpretation of the scene. The events you choose to prioritise will be determined by the *Fabel*.

2. Play the actions described, taking your time over moments of decision.

Engage with the emotional reality of the given circumstances without losing precision.

3. Try the scenario with A as mid-/low-status (5), and B with higher status (7 or 8).

4. Reverse the status roles.

Ask the audience which choices of status best revealed the agreed social significance of the scene.

5. Allow your status to change with circumstances.

This is vitally important, as Brecht was insistent that people are able to change as conditions change. These exercises should *not* lead you to play fixed types: they are there to increase physical articulacy. Any character may embody several status levels in one scene, for example: B may discover that their status is raised when noticing A's desperation. A's status may plummet if they regret extorting money from B. B may simply 'use' a low status to gain sympathy, changing to another when circumstances change.

6. You may discover that choices of status offer new and different 'social significance' to the scene.

If this happens, discuss what is being conveyed and experiment with ways in which you can draw attention to it with clarity and economy.

7. Observers can consider what happens when performers deliberately choose the 'wrong' status.

How does a desperate person appear if they sustain a status level of 9? How does B appear if they sustain a level 3? These reversals of our expectations can produce something jarring, leading to a feeling of unease in the audience. They can make a simple scenario such as this more memorable. This is an example of Brecht's much-talked-about *Verfremdung.*

Transactions like this repeatedly appear in Brecht's plays: in *Mother Courage and Her Children*, Courage haggles over a capon, sells a belt, bargains over ammunition and haggles over the life of her son; in *The Caucasian Chalk Circle*, Grusha is forced to pay an extortionate amount for milk; in *The Good Person of Szechwan*, Shui Ta and Yang Sun sell their shop off for less than its value. Each transaction is financial, but it's also about power, expressed through a status persona (*Gestus*); each exacts a profound cost, both financial and emotional. Each beat in these exchanges requires a particular *Haltung* to illuminate the transactions in money and power and their emotional cost.

Exercise 20. Challenging Archetypal Gestures

Purpose: to look at familiar gestures with fresh eyes.

Here is a series of exercises featuring gestures and actions that are frequently found in classic plays. The exercises are designed to promote selectivity and precision and offer opportunities to explore the vital *Gestic* principle of commentary, by challenging the familiarity of a gesture or action. These exercises can prepare the performer for work in any form of theatre: they increase physical awareness and specificity, reminding the performer that every action contains meaning.

Kneeling in Prayer

Praying devoutly, with dignity, dutifully, reluctantly, insincerely, while doing something else, while thinking something else.

Consider how you kneel down, the tempo, the control, whether the movement is ostentatious, or 'holy', or both. Is there pride in the gesture, or humility? How do you use your hands?

Gestic *commentary on kneeling in prayer*

This is already achieved in the insincere prayer and the one delivered when it is clear that the person's thoughts are elsewhere. Other ways of offering commentary can include:

- Praying as if to perform the devotion to an observer or observers.[32]

- Praying with performed devotion while attempting to hide the performance.
- Praying with such grandeur that the object of worship is the person praying.
- Praying for vengeance with saintly devotion.
- Praying with a devout body and insincerity in the eyes (consider other physical contradictions between pairings of posture, tempo, gesture, gaze and voice).

The Handshake

In pairs, experiment with the following versions of this familiar social gesture.

Find a precise version of the handshakes of:

- Friendship.
- Respect.
- Courtesy.
- Scepticism.
- Distrust.
- Rejection (as if to say 'you may go now').
- Dominance.
- Confidence.
- Attempted neutrality.
- Caution.
- Weakness.

Try a handshake as a conclusion to a business transaction, or a historic moment, such the signing of a peace treaty. Consider which person offers the hand first and why. The person who offers first can be *either* the more powerful in the exchange, demonstrating generosity, or the weaker, attempting ingratiation. The nature of the relationship will reveal the power relations. How long does the handshake go on? Does one party want to end it before the other?

Handshakes and power relations

The above handshakes of rejection and dominance are obvious examples. The gesture can be refined to shed light on a specific power transaction. Here are some examples:

- *Bullying handshakes* – The bully crushes his or her victim's hand while smiling in charming welcome; the bully crushes while nonchalantly looking away; the bully crushes while maintaining eye contact with the victim; the bully crushes while looking away and completes the handshake with eye contact. The victim's choices of response can shed light on the nature of the power exchange: can the victim replace 'victimhood' with astonishment, cool indifference, amusement, steely resistance?
- *Handshakes of snobbery or condescension* – The snob offers a 'wet fish' hand, or just the thumb and fingers, avoiding eye contact. Explore how the snob's body supports or contradicts the handshake. How does the recipient respond?
- *Handshakes of manipulation* – Experiment with ways of playing a warm and generous handshake. What is the rhythm? Do you use both hands, or one? How do you stand? How do you look at the other person? Can you avoid looking 'through' them? Once this is established, how can you reveal that the warmth is manipulative? Is the contradiction in your eyes, stance, body shape or voice?

- *Handshakes of fear* – Imagine you have something in your eye throughout the greeting and struggle to ignore it; imagine your hand is covered in slime as the other person shakes it. In each case, the fear is expressed through the contradiction of attempting to resist it.

The Bow

Find precise versions of this action, experimenting with tempo, depth, and eyeline.

Experiment with the following ways to bow:

- With submission.
- With ingratiation.
- With dignity.
- As an equal.
- With distrust.
- With reluctant respect.
- With no respect.

Gestic *commentary in a bow*

The person bowing may have an ulterior motive; the bow may come at an unexpected moment in the action; the person bowing may be abusing, seducing or tricking the other person. Consider the bow…

- of a defendant to the judge in a corrupt court.
- of a republican to a monarch.
- of a constitutional monarch to parliament.
- of a deposed monarch to a new parliament.

The commentary may also refer to the nature of the event in which the action takes place: the person who bows could feel tense or complacent or experience a sense of foreboding. Drama is full of such moments, and this small gesture can provide arresting preparation for the action that follows it. See the way John Proctor in *The Crucible* and Galileo in Brecht's *The Life of Galileo* acknowledge their interrogators. Likewise, Azdak, as he bows to the lawyers and witnesses in the last scene of *The Caucasian Chalk Circle*; and the principal characters in the trial (Act Four, Scene One) of *The Merchant of Venice*.

Exercise 21. *Gestus* in *Hamlet*[33]

Purpose: to employ Gestus *to reveal social realities and relationships.*

This extract has been adapted from the dumb show during Act Three, Scene Two of Shakespeare's *Hamlet* to suit the needs of the exercise. It comprises a series of physical actions, and each can be played with a particular *Gestus*.

The exercise requires three performers and one reader.

Version I

One person reads out each action, and the other three perform the actions as described. The reader must give time between each stage direction to allow the performers to arrive at a detailed choice of action.

> Enter a King and Queen, the Queen embracing him and he her. She kneels, and makes show of protestation unto him. He takes her up, and declines his head upon her neck. He lies him down upon a bank of flowers. She, seeing him asleep, leaves him. Anon comes in another man, takes off the King's crown, kisses it, pours poison in the sleeper's ears, and leaves him. The Queen returns, finds the King dead, makes

passionate action. The poisoner returns and seems to condole with her. The dead body is carried away. The poisoner woos the Queen with gifts. She seems harsh awhile, but in the end accepts his love.

Version 2

In the group of three, consider the social realities of the scenario: the hierarchy is initially King – Queen – Poisoner. Regicide is a capital offence, and the punishment would be particularly gruesome. None of the conspirators' actions can be played easily. Make *Gestic* choices that articulate the social reality of the scenario. The reader can read out to the performers the suggestions in bold:

Enter a King and Queen,

Their bearing demonstrates their hierarchical relations.

the Queen embracing him and he her.

They are always aware that they can be seen by the public.

She kneels,

Her devotion must seem fervent – but not overdone.

and makes show of protestation unto him.

She is anxious her previous action might have been regarded as insincere.

Or:

She is aware of the poisoner's presence.

He takes her up, and declines his head upon her neck.

Her responses to these actions are important, and become the focus of the moment.

He lies him down upon a bank of flowers.

Their bearing changes from public to private.

She, seeing him asleep, leaves him.

Her departure is a '*Not... But...*' Does she know the poisoner is near? Her terror of the consequences of regicide is vital here.

Anon comes in another man, takes off the King's crown, kisses it,

Does his *Haltung* reveal greed for power or devotion to the role of monarch? The latter would imply that the assassin has principles, and is attempting to replace a bad king.

pours poison in the sleeper's ears, and leaves him.

Is he cautious, reckless or furtive? Is he fast or slow? Is he brazen or surreptitious?

The Queen returns, finds the King dead, makes passionate action.

Does she regret the murder? Is she frightened she will be abandoned by the poisoner?

The poisoner returns

The conspirators face the reality of what they have done: their terror is private.

and seems to condole with her.

The condolence must appear convincing should anyone intrude.

The dead body is carried away.

Now this is a public event. The conspirators perform their mourning.

The poisoner woos the queen with gifts.

He can offer her jewels, or perhaps a crown: each offer sets up a '*Not... But...*' for her.

She seems harsh awhile,

Decide whether this is public or private.

but in the end accepts his love.

And the hierarchical relations change: he is now King.

The Actor and the Director resume their discussion.

ACTOR. So *Gestus* is about making physical choices that comment on social relationships. I'm okay with that, and I get the idea of making customs and clichés unfamiliar. But it's still hard to grasp the idea of playing a part and commenting on it at the same time – even harder to be able to just do it.

DIRECTOR. It's not easy to direct it either. But it was observable in the exercises...

ACTOR. Yes, in an exercise, maybe, but it doesn't come naturally... it goes completely against my instincts.

DIRECTOR. What was useful for you in the exercises?

ACTOR. It's always useful when I avoid focusing on myself.

DIRECTOR. So you're saying that you can comment on what your character is doing if you don't think about commenting on it?

ACTOR. Yes, maybe that's it... the process is counter-intuitive for me. My instinct is to be *inside* my character, not outside it.

DIRECTOR. There is a good example of this in an account of how Brecht directed *The Caucasian Chalk Circle.* The peasant extorts a small fortune from Grusha for a tiny cup of milk, and he then sees her struggling with her pack. Brecht told the actor playing the peasant to help her with it. The actor said such a sudden change didn't seem justified. Brecht asked the actor why they should present only one side to his personality, adding 'people are inclined to dispense kindness when it costs them nothing'.[34]

ACTOR. And in that example, playing the contradiction still allowed the actor stay 'inside' the character.

DIRECTOR. Yes I think so: the act of kindness would be sincere.

The actor says this approach works against his instincts; repeated work on the exercises given so far can address this. They can be supplemented by an exercise on the *Gestus* of showing.

Exercise 22. The *Gestus* of Showing

Purpose: to develop an instinct for showing.

These are exercises to draw attention to the actor's own *Gestus*, rather than that of the character they are playing. In each of these exercises, play or narrate a scene as if it's being performed to a live audience. In each case, the *performance* of the action and story is as important as the story itself.

Any of the archetypal gestures in Exercise 22 can be revisited with one or more of the variations in the following exercise.

1. As Derren Brown

Derren Brown's rapport with the audience means their pleasure from his act comes as much from their knowledge that he is tricking them as it does from the illusions themselves. Revisit some of the handshakes listed above, performing them in this style. This exercise can be used employing scenes in which one character tricks, manipulates or hoodwinks another, such as Iago, Richard III, or Subtle and Face in Ben Jonson's *The Alchemist*, or Volpone and Mosca in Jonson's *Volpone* – in fact, any of the numerous gulling scenes in English comedy.

2. As a celebrity chef

TV chefs want the audience to learn the required culinary skills while simultaneously being impressed with his/her dexterity and with the deliciousness of the food. Play or narrate a scene from an established text while imagining you are a TV chef. Try it first without deciding its 'social significance' – the ensemble can discuss what meanings emerge. Play the scene again with a chosen political challenge in mind, incorporating examples of *Gestus* that emerged in the first version.

3. Crimewatch

The reporter's presence as they walk through the scene surrounding the crime reassures the audience that s/he is dispassionate and responsible. This exercise might be particularly useful with Exercise 16 in this chapter or the arrest narrative in Exercise 9.

Exercise 23. Discovering *Gestic* Commentary Through Contradictory Activities

Purpose: to develop mental and physical awareness of Gestic *possibilities.*

Below is a series of activities that can be performed while playing dialogue. The process of engaging with two realities simultaneously can enable actors to discover how actions can comment on words or intentions. In each case, the activity can challenge a received view of a character.

These exercises can be used in training, in rehearsal, or adapted for directorial interpretation of a scene in performance.

One character shaves another with a cut-throat razor

With thanks to *Sweeney Todd* and Büchner's *Woyzeck* for this idea. It's unlikely that this could be used in performances of the scenes listed below, but in each case the performer can discover new ways to comment on the scene, exploring the mismatch between words and physicality. The barber has the power, but has to move with great care and gentleness; the customer is effectively strait-jacketed. Try it with a mirror and without.

- Iago meticulously and lovingly shaves Othello while subtly kindling the latter's jealousy in Act Three, Scene Three.
- Jamie shaves Matty when the latter visits him in prison in Simon Stephens's *Country Music*.
- Edmund shaves Edgar while tricking him in Act One, Scene Two of *King Lear*.
- Ariel or Tupolski shaves Katurian in Act One, Scene One of *The Pillowman* by Martin McDonagh.

Two characters fold linen together while they argue

This is based on a rare example of a training exercise proposed by Brecht himself. In his version, two women fold linen while feigning an aggressive argument for the benefit of their husbands, who are in an adjoining room.[35] Sustaining the activity helps the performers to control aggressive emotions. The anger becomes contained and focused as it is expressed to support specific intentions.

As well as developing skills in controlling emotion, performers gain skill in playing physical rhythms and tempos that conflict with their emotional drives.

- Emphasise the disjunction between voice and body, and between body and intentions.

- Play the ebb and flow in the struggle between activity and feeling; allow one 'side' to win.
- Find a single moment when voice and body are in harmony. What is the effect of this moment on the spectators? Observers can give feedback on moments in which this mismatch offered insightful commentary on the scene.
- Observers can copy these moments and re-enact them for the original performers. You can record the scenes if this gives greater precision to the copied moves.
- The original performers copy the copied versions of themselves. This can heighten particularly telling gestures and movements.

Any argument scene can be used: it might be those in which the activity conforms with expected gender roles, such as Mother Courage and Yvette's haggling over the cart; scenes from Lorca's *The House of Bernarda Alba*, Angie and Marlene in Caryl Churchill's *Top Girls* – or those that do not, such as the quarrel between all four lovers in *A Midsummer Night's Dream*, or between Brutus and Cassius in *Julius Caesar.*

Other activities for voice–body mismatch

- One character carefully – even lovingly – dresses the other's wounds while they perform a scene of tension or hostility.
- The characters waltz together as they argue.
- Characters mime eating while arguing. Several versions:
  a. One or both characters use their cutlery the wrong way around.

b. Both have to maintain their dignity in the process.

c. Both have to do so with outsized cutlery.[36]

- Play the scene as if you are in a restaurant: one character plays the waiter, the other the customer. (You can reverse the power relations given in the scene.)
- Both engage in a rhythmical work activity, such as cleaning windows or sweeping the floor.

While these exercises increase an actor's physical control and coordination and open up awareness of *Gestic* possibilities, many will release a scene's comic potential.

Below is a series of exercises in which actors can develop awareness of the dialectical possibilities of juxtaposition.

Exercise 24. Juxtaposition

Purpose: to develop awareness of Gestic *commentary through silent responses.*

A delivers a political speech: it can be anything from Enoch Powell's 'Rivers of blood' to Martin Luther King's 'I have a dream'. It can be Brutus's or Mark Antony's speeches to the citizens in *Julius Caesar*, or Joan of Arc's speech from Shakespeare's *Henry VI, Part 1*.

B sits on the opposite side of the stage, with a full glass of water or beer. It is as if B is watching A's speech on a screen in front of him. Try the speech several times: B can react spontaneously and honestly as s/he hears the speech, possibly punctuating the speech by drinking, or stopping her/himself from doing so if s/he hears something that affects her/him.

- The ensemble watches and discusses the nature of the comment made by B's actions. Discuss how B's actions can:

a. Support the content of the speech.

b. Call to question its content.

c. Draw attention to particular arguments or phrases.

- Consider too how A's timing, gesture and tempo can enrich B's contributions.

B can be a prison convict (either fictional or based on a real person) watching the Home Secretary's speech on the effectiveness of prison, or on the need for Prison Reform.

B can be a squaddie listening to a politician or to Colonel Tim Collins' famous speech to the troops in the first Iraq war.[37]

The presence of an onstage audience can often guide or challenge an audience's response to a public event. Brecht asked the soldiers in his production of *Mother Courage and Her Children* to respond with astonishment at Courage's hardness when she is shown Swiss Cheese's corpse.

Exercise 25. Silent Performers

Purpose: to develop awareness of Gestic *possibilities of juxtaposition between two silent performers.*

A and B represent opposite sides in a conflict, and they listen silently to news of an important event, such as an election, the outcome of a war, a peace negotiation (this could be from a news broadcast or from a script). It helps if the announcement lasts at least forty-five seconds, and ideally two or three minutes. Possible scenarios:

- A is a victim of the accused, and B is the mother of the accused. They listen to news of the jury's verdict, the judge's comments and the passing of the sentence.

a. Establish the nature of the crime, its history and the nature of the relationships involved.

b. An internet source can be used, but thorough research into the trial is necessary before using these sources.

- A is a refugee already resident in a host country, and B is a person who feels threatened by the influx of migrants in an area with scarce resources. They await news on whether members of the refugee's family will be granted admission to the country.
- A is a Palestinian and B is a Zionist. They listen to a Pathé broadcast in which the votes are counted for and against a partition plan that would favour the Zionists.[38] The remarkable nature of the broadcast is that as each country's name is called their representative must declare their vote by saying 'Yes', 'No' or 'Abstain'. The listeners will have a specific response both to the country voting and to their vote. They also count the votes for their side. By the end they will know the outcome before it is announced.
- A Remain and a Leave voter listen to the outcome of the Brexit Referendum.[39]

1. Allow some time for A and B to enter the world of the scenario, waiting for the announcement to begin or for the result to be confirmed. They might pace, breathe heavily, sit or stand very still, etc.
2. Run the broadcast or read the announcements. A and B listen and respond without looking at each other. The audience note striking moments in the interplay of their responses.
3. Rerun the announcement with A and B looking at each other. Incorporate and develop their immediate responses

in stage 1 with responses to what they see when looking at each other.

4. Rerun the announcement, pausing its presentation after key sentences or phrases, giving A and B a chance to physically refine or extend their responses. This stage can be worked initially with actors looking at each other, and then without doing so.
5. Observers can show particularly striking physical expressions, demonstrating how they were timed with those of the other performer. Each performer can copy and sharpen their presentation of the observer's version.
6. Optional: deliver a new announcement, this time reversing the verdict given in the first version. Follow this with stages 2 to 5.

The process of repeating, refining, timing *and copying* each gesture enables the performers to embody emotional experience and simultaneously *stand outside* and show it to the audience.

Gestic Arrangements

Brecht's view of humans as social animals is manifest in the way so much of the action of his plays takes place in open, public spaces. Even ostensibly private scenes between individuals have a public – and therefore political – dimension. Those groups or crowds who observe the events he dramatises in his plays are never mere observers: they are part of the society in which the events take place, influencing its outcome and experiencing its consequences. These exercises are designed to increase an ensemble's awareness of the *Gestic* potential of a group or crowd that is both participant and observer.

Exercise 26. The Cinema Audience

Purpose: to explore socially influenced responses.

Group A, comprising half of the ensemble, creates a short non-verbal Hitchcock-style 'film clip' to be watched by the other half of the group. In this exercise, the onstage audience are more important the the 'onscreen' performers. The clip can be structured as follows:

1. The victim is engaged in an activity, unaware of the assailant's presence.
2. The assailant enters the house and moves towards the victim.
3. The assailant draws and prepares the murder weapon.
4. The victim sees the assailant, dives for cover.
5. The weapon misses its target.
6. Silence.
7. Both hide.
8. The victim attempts to escape; the murderer stalks.
9. The victim knocks something or gives away his/her presence.
10. The murderer attacks the victim.
11. The death is bloody.
12. The murderer escapes silently.

The other half of the ensemble (Group B) comprises one or more of the following:

- The filmmaker.
- The film's principal investor.
- A producer.

- A film critic.
- A connoisseur of murder films.
- An obsessive fan of the actor playing the victim.
- An equally obsessive fan of the actor playing the assailant.
- A squeamish person who may have been brought to the event by one of the above.
- A sociologist/psychologist interested in studying how groups behave when observing violence.

Once the film is rehearsed, the observers can watch several times. Those members of Group A that don't perform in the clip each observe an individual from Group B.

1. First screening: the watchers express their responses both vocally and from their seated positions. The workshop leader gives feedback to the audience on what s/he noticed.
2. Second screening: with the feedback in mind, the watchers either extend or refine their responses.
3. Third screening: the seating is removed and the watchers can express their responses using their whole body and can move in the space. The workshop leader gives feedback.
4. Fourth screening: following feedback, the responses are extended or refined.
5. Fifth screening: the observers from Group A perform what they saw to the original audience.
6. For the final screening, the workshop leader or observers can arrange the audience members so as to heighten the contrasts or contradictions in their responses. Consider here your *standpoint*: in what way do you wish to comment

on the event and its observers? This careful arrangement of contrasting groups is a vital element in Brecht's staging of his own plays.

The exercise demonstrates the multiplicity of responses an event can elicit while also showing how individual responses are influenced by class, occupation, personal interest or other socially constructed attitudes. The exercise shows how the *Gestic* expression of these responses can communicate a standpoint or range of positions on an event and the society in which it takes place.

Conclusion

In the second part of this chapter, I will refer to scenes in famous plays in which an onstage audience is present. These include trial scenes from *The Merchant of Venice*, *The Winter's Tale* and *The Crucible.* I will also refer to the way the characters on stage respond to the 'breaking string' in Chekhov's *The Cherry Orchard.*

The above are training exercises that can be repeated to enable performers to refine their *Gestic* vocabulary. Part two of this chapter comprises textual extracts demonstrating the ways this approach can illuminate particular scenes.

Gestus: Part Two

Using Gestus *in Specific Scenes*

Exercise 27. Using Objects as *Gestic* Commentary

The Keys

In Chekhov's *The Cherry Orchard*, Varya drops the Ranevsky estate keys to the floor after Lopakhin has announced that he is the new owner. Lopakhin notes this, and the text says that he picks them up and jingles them. The archetypal power of keys as a symbol of hope, home, the past and the future was brought home to me in Jalazon refugee camp in the occupied territories of Palestine, when young people showed me the keys to their grandparents' former homes in the old city of Jaffa. Consider the possible commentary that is made by various ways in which Lopakhin handles the keys. These might include:

- Throwing the keys in the air in triumph.
- Throwing the keys in the air but then dropping them.
- Gazing at them in wonder and awe.
- Sliding them into his pocket without thinking.
- Lampooning Varya by displaying them as if dangling from a chain.

Observers can consider and advise on the impact of any one of these choices.

The Title Deeds to the Estate

Lopakhin could be holding the title deed to the property during this scene: Ranevskaya could snatch it from him immediately after he announces that he bought the estate. Does she stare at it in disbelief, tear it in despair, return it to him, or let it fall from her hands? Each gesture offers commentary on property, class and power at that moment in history.

In this scene, Chekhov already gives practitioners an opportunity to stage the scene dialectically, placing the heartbroken Ranevskaya on one side while Lopakhin delivers his account of the sale on the other. The juxtaposition reflects the conflicting class interests, and the emotional cost of an event that is part of a seismic social change on a historic scale. The timing of her responses can shift an audience's perception of the event. The performer can undermine an audience's perception of Ranevskaya as a weak victim if she strikes Lopakhin when he asks her why she didn't listen to her.

Exercise 28. *Gestic* Arrangement as Commentary

These exercises follow on from the *Gestic* ensemble exercise in the previous chapter.

As we have seen, the groupings within a scene, or the 'arrangement' as Brecht calls them, convey a particular social or political standpoint – shedding light on both an event and on the society in which it takes place. To achieve the latter, an onstage audience should be seen as a play's society in miniature.

Gestic arrangement in response to the 'Breaking String'

Purpose: to use Haltung *in a group's response, creating a* Gestic *arrangement to an event, drawing attention to its significance.*

In Act Two of *The Cherry Orchard*, the characters sit lost in thought as they watch the sun set over the estate. Most of them have been contemplating the happy and painful moments of their past and the frightening prospect of their future. Suddenly a sound is heard in the distance that seems to come from the sky and which Chekhov describes as the sound of a 'breaking string'. Directors often labour for hours with sound designers in search of the right effect: the noise represents something akin to W. B. Yeats' 'terrible beauty' in his poem 'Easter 1916' in which all is 'changed, changed utterly'. In some productions, the moment resembles an earthquake, others use something percussive with reverb, others imitate the sound of a distant mining cable breaking. Whatever the choice, it is odd that few productions explore the impact of the noise on the characters.

Preparation

1. Each actor can consider their character's greatest fear, first whispering it to themselves, describing in detail the events as they unfold. They can attempt to make the same description only in intoned sound, then expressing it silently through the tempo of their walk.
2. Each actor can then focus on their character's view of the future: for some it might involve a miracle; for others, a new political order; for others, bankruptcy; for others, a new future in another place. They can explore it in the same way that they considered their greatest fear in stage 1.
3. Before they hear the sound, the actors alternate their attention between stages 1 and 2 above.

Experimenting with responses to the 'breaking string'

4. Tell the actors that they can move towards the sound, away from it, remain seated, or stand up. Their response is a spontaneous interaction between the sound and the thoughts already in their minds.
5. Play the sound and allow the actors to respond in the space for as long as possible before returning to the dialogue.
6. Repeat 3 and 5 above, but this time performers can give their attention to the other characters, allowing their responses and movements to influence their own.

Observations

This exercise often reveals interesting responses: I have seen Lopakhin stride towards the noise, a man of action willing to deal with an industrial accident; Trofimov move slowly and thoughtfully towards it, the scientist fascinated by its mystery; Ranevskaya reach to pull her children close, or recoil terrified; Anya weep at the sight of her helpless mother; Varya pray feverishly; Firs wake with a snort and a joyless laugh.

Gestic **arrangement and Shylock's 'Pound of Flesh'**

Purpose: to experiment with group Gestus *to expose the prevailing attitudes in a play's society.*

The trial scene in Shakespeare's *Merchant of Venice*, with its vengeful Jew sharpening his knife, its 'quality of mercy' speech and its near-death moment for Antonio, is certainly spectacular melodrama. It is also the scene in which the moral and social values of the state of Venice are laid bare. Working on *Gestic* social groupings can offer opportunities to make incisive comment on these social and moral currents.

1. Identifying separate interest groups

A large-cast production will give representation to the range of interest groups in the scene, so in addition to the lawyers and witnesses, these include:

- *The Duke* – he should appear inscrutable, although he is explicit when it comes to his disgust for Shylock's absolutism.
- *The Magnificoes* – these are eminent persons who have achieved their position by attaining great wealth. Participating in public events can offer advancement for them personally, financially and socially.
- *Antonio's friends* – including Bassanio, Gratiano and Salerio.
- *The anti-Semitic citizenry* (comprising men and women) – they can be separated to reveal their various and contrasting responses.
- *Shylock's associates* – each wears a yellow disc, marking them as Jews.
- *Guards* – charged with preventing disorder between hostile observers.
- *Clergy* – they may be called upon to bless the proceedings and even offer moral guidance.

2. Establishing group identities

A workshop leader asks the group to establish the hierarchy of this sample of Venetian society. If one end of the room represents the highest, and the opposite the lowest, each grouping can place itself in that spectrum, in relation to the following hierarchies:

- Wealth.
- Power.

- Social status.
- Self-esteem.

They should find that a high position in one hierarchy does not guarantee the same position in another. The final one – self-esteem – is the least easy to establish uncontroversially, but it could be the most interesting.

3. Arrangement

The director, designer and company can design a courtroom, reflecting the above, juxtaposing those groups that represent rival positions in the pecking order.

4. Orchestrating Gestic *responses*

With the workshop leader functioning like an orchestral conductor, s/he can bring in or silence each group's response to a particular moment. The conductor can encourage a group to respond vocally, or silently, or by standing, sitting or moving. Here are a few sample moments with comments:

a. The Duke's opening remarks:

> Shylock, the world thinks, and I think so too,
> That thou but lead'st this fashion of thy malice
> To the last hour of act; and then 'tis thought
> Thou'lt show thy mercy and remorse more strange
> Than is thy strange apparent cruelty;

Here, the Jews' responses in the public gallery might convey quiet bitterness that no such mercy is afforded them in their everyday lives. The Venetian citizens may be divided: some may be willing Shylock to follow the Duke's suggestion: others may simply regard Shylock with disgust.

b. Shylock can point at various members of the onstage audience when he says:

> Some men there are love not a gaping pig;
> Some, that are mad if they behold a cat;
> And others, when the bagpipe sings i' the nose,
> Cannot contain their urine: for affection,
> Mistress of passion, sways it to the mood
> Of what it likes or loathes.

Some of the more sophisticated of the Magnificoes may enjoy the irony of Shylock's taunts; the citizens themselves may become restive or even angry as the speech continues; the guards may have to restore order. Since racial prejudice is approved by political and ecclesiastical authority, the guards may blame the Jews for disorder in court and deal with them harshly.

c. Antonio, refers to Shylock, saying:

> You may as well do anything most hard,
> As seek to soften that – than which what's harder?
> His Jewish heart.

See previous note. This rabble-rousing line comes from the meekest man in court. Perhaps the clergy might pray for the Jew's conversion, while Jews in the public gallery can protest, remain silent, or brace themselves for an onslaught. Some Magnificoes could take a populist position, joining the rabble; others could choose to appear statesmanlike.

d. Bassanio and Gratiano say they would be prepared to sacrifice their wives to save Antonio:

> BASSANIO.
> Antonio, I am married to a wife
> Which is as dear to me as life itself;

But life itself, my wife, and all the world,
Are not with me esteem'd above thy life:
I would lose all, ay, sacrifice them all
Here to this devil, to deliver you.

PORTIA.
Your wife would give you little thanks for that,
If she were by, to hear you make the offer.

GRATIANO.
I have a wife, whom, I protest, I love:
I would she were in heaven, so she could
Entreat some power to change this currish Jew.

NERISSA.
'Tis well you offer it behind her back;
The wish would make else an unquiet house.

Consider the contrasting responses of the men and women in the public gallery.

The instances above are a few sample moments. The point is to consider how such responses can be woven into the fabric of the scene.

- Individual sectors can be given prominence.
- Hostilities can be dramatised and suppressed.
- Action can be slowed or quickened to draw attention to a particular choice.
- Sections of the crowd and the speaking characters can play off each other.

These ensemble responses could be presented as reaction shots in a screen version of the play; equally, they could be used as provocations for the main characters in a rehearsal-room exercise. But this would miss Brecht's point: the scene shows the kind of place that Venice is, revealing the relationship between the state and its populace. The observing groups aren't extras, they are people. Their responses animate the scene and expand its scope. The reactions could be internalised, charging the scene with suppressed energy, a palpable manifestation of the dynamics of an oppressive state. At moments, collective discord or humour could erupt, adding vividness to the depiction of the trial as a reflection of Venetian society.

These exercises can be adapted to suit any scene that takes place in the public sphere, whether it is the choric responses to the *Agon* of a Greek tragedy, the hearings and trial of *The Crucible*, Shaw's *Saint Joan*, Hermione's trial in *The Winter's Tale*, or the public speeches of Brutus and Mark Antony in *Julius Caesar*.

Exercise 29. *Gestus* and the Proposal that Didn't Happen

Purpose: to use Gestic *responses to show the influence of class on the outcome of significant events.*

By the final act of *The Cherry Orchard*, the estate has been sold and Varya faces a bleak future as a spinster housekeeper for the Ragulin family. She needs Lopakhin to propose marriage to recover her fortunes.

A perfectly acceptable choice would be for the actor playing Varya to play the scene desperately wanting Lopakhin to propose: this would probably make her behaviour awkward, anxious and passive as she nervously waits for him to make his move. It certainly fits with her tears of despair at the end of the scene when he leaves without proposing.

The way Ranevskaya sets up the proposal makes both Lopakhin and Varya self-conscious: can there be anything less romantic than being asked to agree to a marriage in short order while people listen in, giggling behind the door? It is precisely these circumstances that make it more likely that Varya would notice everything that is off-putting about Lopakhin: his vulgar materialism, his opportunism, and the way he destroyed the Ranevsky estate; the way his rapacious obsession with work renders him asexual, leaving him no room to experience or express attraction to women; his 'peasant' social awkwardness; his apparent lack of religious spirituality.

The performer playing Varya can be aware of these characteristics as she works on the scene, commenting on them aloud as she sees them become manifest through his actions. She can play *Gestus* of repulsion, and Lopakhin's actor may find it impossible to propose in the face of such tacit rejection. Simultaneously, a marriage to Lopakhin would be financially advantageous, and he allegedly loves her. There may be moments in the scene in which Varya clings to these realities, momentarily changing the rhythm and direction of the scene. A *Gestic* exploration of this contradiction can makes Varya active in the events that shape her life, demonstrating how class-bound values and attitudes can influence its direction.

Exercise 30. *Gestus* and Gertrude's Contradiction

Purpose: to use the 'Not… But…' *as* Gestic *commentary on the personal, moral and social forces that influence a character's choice of action.*

In many productions of *Hamlet*, Gertrude in Act Three, Scene Four, responds in distressed agony to Hamlet's onslaught, to the extent that she cries out at Hamlet's 'rank sweat of an enseamed bed' speech. She is similarly distraught when confessing that he has 'cleft [her] heart in twain'. This reading is perfectly justified by the text but makes it difficult to reveal *why* she stays with Claudius in the face of such an assault on her conscience.

There is a practical justification for Gertrude's choice of second husband. On the one hand, marrying Claudius is a viable survival strategy for the wife of a murdered monarch in a ruthless and corrupt patriarchy. With this as her primary motivation, she could persuade herself that Hamlet's condemnations come from the hysteria of a young man unable to accept his mother's new lover and husband.

On the other hand, she acknowledges her guilt ('Thou turn'st my eyes in to my very soul, / And there I see such black and grained spots / As will not leave their tinct'). The line in which she says her 'heart is cleft in twain' expresses this contradiction. As a mother, she feels profound pity and sympathy for her son; as a survivor at court, she must stay focused on maintaining a self-protective alliance with Claudius.

She can play *Gestus* of pity and sympathy for her son, tough rejection of Hamlet's expressions of disgust towards Claudius, and ultimately of a triumph of her will over sentiment. The actor playing Gertrude can employ a '*Not... But...*' emphasising the moral and emotional cost of each of her decisions. In this way, careful *Gestic* choices can reveal that her decision comes from the conditions in which she has to survive.

Exercise 31. *Gestus* and Social Class in *Twelfth Night*

Purpose: to use Gestus *to reveal how social rank influences thought and behaviour in a comic encounter.*

The architecture of Shakespeare's open-air theatres demanded physical articulacy. With no lights to give the focus to an individual character and a minimum of design elements, the actor appears as a figure in space. The performer has a responsibility to define the outlines of that figure with precision.

The famous first encounter between Olivia and Viola in *Twelfth Night* (Act One, Scene Five) gains a lively and provocative dimension if its class relations and identities are revealed through the actors' *Gestic* choices. Viola's disguise disrupts expected class relations and sets them at a distance; her successful performance as a boy simultaneously provokes Olivia's unwitting homosexual attraction. (The sexuality of the scene would have been unsettling in Elizabethan England, where sodomy was a capital offence, and given that both characters would have been played by boys.)

Notes on class identities

- Viola is actually an aristocratic lady, but she is in disguise as a young male page. Olivia is the daughter of a count. Each performer needs to identify and establish their character's essential *Gestic* identity.
- Viola externally plays the page – a servant in rank but, in Tudor times, usually an apprentice knight, so a person of breeding.
- Viola's actor can choose when she betrays her femininity and when to maintain her masculine *Haltung*. This is complicated by the higher social status attached to her feminine self and the deference required of a page. The performer will need to define with clarity her two selves, i.e. Cesario's deference and maleness, and Viola's femininity, ease and entitlement.
- Viola's love for Orsino can make her jealous of Olivia's beauty, producing a contradiction between her male *Haltung* and her inner jealousy.

Here follows the scene in full, with notes preceding each event in this typeface, and annotations on class and *Gestic* choices in italic.

Event 1. Covering up before meeting the messenger

The Countess Olivia prepares to hear the Duke Orsino's message of wooing. She and her waiting gentlewoman Maria cover their faces.

Gestic considerations: Olivia and Maria's *Gestus* reveal their class difference, in contrast with their performance after Viola enters.

OLIVIA.
Give me my veil: come, throw it o'er my face.
We'll once more hear Orsino's embassy.

Event 2. Who is who?

Viola enters disguised as a page and asks which is the lady, since both women are seated and veiled.

Gestic considerations: Viola's rehearsed physical rhythms are disrupted by her confusion as to which woman is the lady of the house.

Enter VIOLA *and Attendants.*

VIOLA.
The honourable lady of the house, which is she?

Maria pretends to be someone who could be taken for the lady of the house; her Haltung *doesn't give away her inferior class; both sit identically; both are veiled.*

Viola's Gestus *can reveal her surprise at Olivia's trick – which has disrupted class relations. Viola can interrupt her bow of greeting, registering her shock at the unexpected arrangement of the women. Her serving-woman doesn't stand in attendance, but sits beside her in disguise as a lady. She could then make her bow again – a double-take around a bow.*

OLIVIA.
Speak to me; I shall answer for her. Your will?

Olivia could ask this question because Viola's bafflement has left her tongue-tied.

Event 3. What role are you playing?

Confusion and curiosity over identities repeatedly interrupts Viola's delivery of Orsino's message.

Gestic considerations: Each interruption to Viola's speech of praise challenges the disguise; she momentarily forgets herself when she criticises Olivia's refusal to accept a suitor. Each moment requires precise *Gestic* definition: to what extent is the disguise dropped? Initial rehearsals should involve a complete contrast between her two selves, like the difference between Shen Te and Shui Ta in *The Good Person of Szechwan*.

VIOLA. Most radiant, exquisite and unmatchable beauty – I pray you, tell me if this be the lady of the house, for I never saw her: I would be loath to cast away my speech, for besides that it is excellently well penned, I have taken great pains to con it. Good beauties, let me sustain no scorn; I am very comptible, even to the least sinister usage.

OLIVIA. Whence came you, sir?

VIOLA. I can say little more than I have studied, and that question's out of my part. Good gentle one, give me modest assurance if you be the lady of the house, that I may proceed in my speech.

OLIVIA. Are you a comedian?

VIOLA. No, my profound heart:

Viola's Gestic *response is to say 'I certainly do not belong to the vagabond caste.'*

and yet, by the very fangs of malice I swear, I am not that I play. Are you the lady of the house?

Viola's aristocratic patience is tested: she has to repeat her question.

OLIVIA. If I do not usurp myself, I am.

VIOLA. Most certain, if you are she, you do usurp yourself; for what is yours to bestow is not yours to reserve.

A relatively lowly page is telling the daughter of a count how she should behave in her own house. Olivia is both outraged and fascinated.

But this is from my commission: I will on with my speech in your praise, and then show you the heart of my message.

OLIVIA. Come to what is important in't: I forgive you the praise.

VIOLA. Alas, I took great pains to study it, and 'tis poetical.

OLIVIA. It is the more like to be feigned: I pray you, keep it in.

Event 4. This is rudeness

Olivia upbraids Viola/Cesario for his impertinence. Maria tries to remove Viola; Viola wins the power struggle.

Gestic considerations: Viola's female *Gestic* persona is probably more effective in her power struggle with Maria.

OLIVIA. I heard you were saucy at my gates, and allowed your approach rather to wonder at you than to hear you. If you be not mad, be gone; if you have reason, be brief: 'tis not that time of moon with me to make one in so skipping a dialogue.

To Olivia, impertinence from a person of servant class is a sign of madness.

MARIA. Will you hoist sail, sir? here lies your way.

VIOLA. No, good swabber; I am to hull here a little longer. Some mollification for your giant, sweet lady. Tell me your mind: I am a messenger.

Maria calls Viola 'sir', casting him as captain of the ship that she will escort from this port. Viola accepts the position of ship captain and positions Maria as a lowly deck-swabber. This is the only time she addresses Maria directly. Viola's Gestus *here is that of an aristocrat dismissing a servant.*

When talking to Olivia she refers to Maria as a 'giant', a class-based put-down. Now the Gestus *is one of high-born lady addressing an equal. Note that 'sweet lady' immediately follows 'giant'.*

Viola returns to her role as page so that she can assert her right to complete her commission.

> OLIVIA. Sure, you have some hideous matter to deliver, when the courtesy of it is so fearful. Speak your office.
>
> VIOLA. It alone concerns your ear. I bring no overture of war, no taxation of homage: I hold the olive in my hand; my words are as full of peace as matter.
>
> OLIVIA. Yet you began rudely. What are you? What would you?
>
> VIOLA. The rudeness that hath appeared in me have I learned from my entertainment. What I am, and what I would, are as secret as maidenhead; to your ears, divinity, to any other's, profanation.
>
> OLIVIA. Give us the place alone: we will hear this divinity.
>
> *Exeunt* MARIA *and Attendants.*

Maria has been defeated in her power struggle with Viola. Her Gestic *responses can both register her defeat and astonishment at the way Olivia has acted so unexpectedly. Viola might not even acknowledge Maria as she exits.*

Event 5. Partial unmasking

Olivia's repeated ridicule of Orsino's suit stirs Viola's jealousy; the latter needs to know who this woman is that could possibly reject the Duke. She asks to see her face, a request that shocks Olivia. Viola offers to woo Olivia on Orsino's behalf. Her language intensifies Olivia's attraction.

Gestic considerations: the *Haltungen* of a power struggle give way to those of romantic obsession; the audience sees a young woman disguised as a page, while Olivia sees a beautiful young man. Viola's comments are those of a jealous female rival, but Olivia hears them from a fascinating young man. The actor playing Viola calibrates the *Gestus* of her performance with these ironies in mind. Later in the scene, Viola asserts her class identity through the disguise, rather than by dropping it.

OLIVIA. Now, sir, what is your text?

VIOLA. Most sweet lady, –

OLIVIA. A comfortable doctrine, and much may be said of it. Where lies your text?

VIOLA. In Orsino's bosom.

OLIVIA. In his bosom! In what chapter of his bosom?

VIOLA. To answer by the method, in the first of his heart.

OLIVIA. O, I have read it: it is heresy. Have you no more to say?

VIOLA. Good madam, let me see your face.

OLIVIA. Have you any commission from your lord to negotiate with my face? You are now out of your text:

Here Olivia reiterates the point that this boy has overstepped the mark by breaking with class obligations. This outrage nevertheless charms Olivia.

but we will draw the curtain and show you the picture. (*Unveiling.*) Look you, sir, such a one I was this present: is't not well done?

VIOLA. Excellently done, if God did all.

OLIVIA. 'Tis in grain, sir; 'twill endure wind and weather.

VIOLA.
'Tis beauty truly blent, whose red and white
Nature's own sweet and cunning hand laid on:
Lady, you are the cruell'st she alive,
If you will lead these graces to the grave
And leave the world no copy.

Viola switches to verse and speaks with heartfelt sincerity and feminine jealousy.The actor has a Gestic *choice here: she could play this as a page, showing the audience what Olivia sees, or her wonder at her rival's beauty could make her forget her role, revealing her true class and gender.*

OLIVIA. O, sir,

This exclamation shows Olivia revealing her attraction for a moment before shifting to sarcasm.

I will not be so hard-hearted; I will give out divers schedules of my beauty: it shall be inventoried, and every particle and utensil labelled to my will: as, item, two lips, indifferent red; item, two grey eyes, with lids to them; item, one neck, one chin, and so forth. Were you sent hither to praise me?

VIOLA.
I see you what you are, you are too proud;
But, if you were the devil, you are fair.
My lord and master loves you: O, such love
Could be but recompensed, though you were crown'd
The nonpareil of beauty!

Olivia's sarcasm can be a bitter comment on the way her beauty is commodified in the financial arrangements of aristocratic marriage. Viola sustains this image by using the financial term 'recompensed' in her reply.

OLIVIA.

How does he love me?

VIOLA.

With adorations, fertile tears,
With groans that thunder love, with sighs of fire.

OLIVIA.

Your lord does know my mind; I cannot love him:
Yet I suppose him virtuous, know him noble,
Of great estate, of fresh and stainless youth;
In voices well divulged, free, learn'd and valiant;
And in dimension and the shape of nature
A gracious person: but yet I cannot love him;
He might have took his answer long ago.

VIOLA.

If I did love you in my master's flame,
With such a suffering, such a deadly life,
In your denial I would find no sense;
I would not understand it.

OLIVIA.

Why, what would you?

VIOLA.

Make me a willow cabin at your gate,
And call upon my soul within the house;
Write loyal cantons of contemned love
And sing them loud even in the dead of night;
Halloo your name to the reverberate hills
And make the babbling gossip of the air
Cry out 'Olivia!' O, you should not rest
Between the elements of air and earth,
But you should pity me!

Viola's exquisite lines are clearly an expression of her feelings for the Duke. She could attempt to play this with the Gestus *of a male lover, using her disguise to cover her feelings for Orsino. This can give her performance a forcefulness that Olivia interprets as male passion.*

OLIVIA.

You might do much.

What is your parentage?

After Viola's speech, during which Olivia clearly falls for 'Cesario', Olivia's performer can decide how much she gives away when playing the line 'You might do much'. In the question that follows, the Gestus *is that of an heiress considering a suitor.*

VIOLA.

Above my fortunes, yet my state is well:
I am a gentleman.

Viola initially speaks cryptically then asserts her status as a 'gentleman'. Viola asserts her class because it is important to her sense of self-worth; Olivia continues to assess a potential suitor.

OLIVIA.

Get you to your lord;
I cannot love him: let him send no more;
Unless, perchance, you come to me again,
To tell me how he takes it. Fare you well:
I thank you for your pains: spend this for me.

Olivia certainly can't love Orsino now – and that's why she says this. She has to deliver the line differently from easy dismissiveness of the way she delivers the same words earlier in the scene. Now she is absolutely in earnest, which she underlines by offering the page a tip. Her Gestus *is one of aristocratic condescension and deliberate sexuality.*

VIOLA.

I am no fee'd post, lady; keep your purse:

Two examples of Social Gestus*: the aristocrat tips the page flirtatiously; the page is an aristocrat who recoils at the prospect of being paid.*

My master, not myself, lacks recompense.
Love make his heart of flint that you shall love;
And let your fervour, like my master's, be
Placed in contempt! Farewell, fair cruelty.

Exit.

Event 6. Olivia's private thoughts are still public

Gestic considerations: by making her quote from the preceding exchange, Shakespeare is demanding 'Brechtian' acting from Olivia. This is literally 'acting in quotation marks', as she imitates her questioning and Viola's 'male' *Gestus*. This is a private scenic moment, changing her physicality; it is also a public theatrical moment as she delivers lines to an audience.

OLIVIA.
'What is your parentage?'
'Above my fortunes, yet my state is well:
I am a gentleman.' I'll be sworn thou art;
Thy tongue, thy face, thy limbs, actions and spirit
Do give thee five-fold blazon: not too fast: soft, soft!
Unless the master were the man. How now!
Even so quickly may one catch the plague?
Methinks I feel this youth's perfections
With an invisible and subtle stealth
To creep in at mine eyes. Well, let it be.

Olivia can perform an 'action replay' of how she inquired of Viola's parentage, and imitate the Haltungen *of Viola's disguise when she quotes her response. She can wordlessly comment on her own conduct. Now that Olivia is alone, the social 'mask' of control can fall away. We have seen her struggle to maintain it throughout the scene, and there have been moments where she has been caught out. Now in 'private', she thrills in appreciation of the young man. Brecht might nevertheless remind Olivia's actor that she is still in public, since she is addressing a theatre audience. The actor can consider what that audience represents to Olivia: are they social equals, inferiors, or a mixture of the two? Are they the audience of today or Olivia's period in history? What is revealed if we see Olivia releasing her private self and then modifying it as she remembers the presence of an audience?*

Conclusion

Writing the discussions of scenes with *Gestus* constantly in mind has forced me to look at each scene in new ways, interrogating possible meanings while never taking events for granted. While the approach involves considering how social positions and standpoints can be made visible, it never neglects inner life. I would go so far as to say that it enriches it, providing provocations to both performer and character. These tensions between a performer's inner and outer life are explored further in the next chapter.

Emotion

5

Epic theatre... appeals less to the spectators' emotions than to their reason. The spectator is not supposed to share in the experiences of the characters but to question them.

Bertolt Brecht, 'The Epic Theatre and Its Difficulties'[40]

Is it not monstrous that this player here,
But in a fiction, in a dream of passion,
Could force his soul so to his whole conceit
That from her working all his visage wann'd,
Tears in his eyes, distraction in his aspect,
A broken voice, and his whole function suiting
With forms to his conceit? And all for nothing!
For Hecuba!
What's Hecuba to him, or he to Hecuba,
That he should weep for her?

Hamlet, *Act Two, Scene Two*

Hamlet's comment 'And all for nothing!' might have struck a chord with the young Brecht of the late 1920s and early 1930s. He also might have grimaced at Hamlet's assertion that if the player had been prompted by Hamlet's own revenge motive, he would 'drown the stage with tears': he would have regarded such a deluge of despair as an abysmally impotent protest against corruption in Elsinore. Observing empathetic tears in the eyes of an audience, Brecht went further, condemning emotional manipulation as positively dangerous. Hitler's mesmeric power over the German people was powerful evidence that manipulation through empathy resulted in a nation willingly enslaving itself to a monster.

ACTOR. This is one of the most counter-intuitive things about Brecht. Emotion is the lifeblood of theatre. Audiences have to care about what they see and actors have to identify with the characters they play. It seems like Brecht wants us to act badly.

DIRECTOR. I sometimes think that too, but his position changed all the time. Buried in the appendix to his 'Short Organum' of 1949 is this:

'However dogmatic it may seem to warn that empathy with the character should be avoided... however they might follow this advice, they can hardly follow it to the letter, and that is how we are most likely to get that truly rending contradiction between experience and portrayal, empathy and demonstration, justification and criticism, which is what is required.'[41]

ACTOR. Right, so he realised he was wrong all along! I think we are entitled to an apology! Why didn't he admit this before? Why didn't he just dump all the theories that came before this? He only had to read his own plays: they're stuffed with moments when characters cry out or have tears in their eyes. If he writes emotions, then he shouldn't be surprised if actors try to play them!

DIRECTOR. Well, he was already revising his position on emotion in *The Messingkauf Dialogues*, which were mostly written the

1940s. He was even more open about the value of feeling when he returned to Germany after the war. At this point he could test his theories in a state-funded theatre company.

ACTOR. So when he actually worked on his plays, and saw the actors engaging emotionally, he realised that emotion was perfectly valid.

DIRECTOR. He isn't that easy to pin down. He said it was his writing style that was misleading. But yes, he wanted the actor to live inside the character and stand outside it.

ACTOR. So he wants it both ways: feeling and commenting at the same time. I'm not convinced that is possible – and even if it is, how do we decide on which emotions are allowed and which are not?

Readers of this book may have had or heard conversations like this. We could respond to it by saying that Brecht wanted to put emotion *to work*, rather than present it for its own sake. He envisaged it as part of a theatrical language that could reveal an event's underlying causes. I was once given the advice: 'If it's already red, don't paint it red.' In other words, when you're in an emotionally powerful scene, avoid coating it with *more* emotion. The narration of a tragic event gains emotional power if it is narrated dispassionately – or at least if we observe the speaker controlling their emotions. The events then remain the focus, rather than the private anguish of the narrator. The same can apply to action as well as narrative. In the exercises below, we show how emotion can be regulated in this way.

They also deal with ways to select and calibrate a scene's emotional content to achieve a simultaneous tension between feeling and commentary. I will discuss ways to choreograph emotions, using feeling as one of several means of theatrical communication, organised to promote a dialectical way of seeing:

> In reality we are of course dealing with two mutually hostile processes that are combined in the actors' work (their performances do not just contain a bit of the one and a bit of the other). The actors derive their true effectiveness from the tussle and tension of the two opposites.[42]

So indeed Brecht is saying to actors: 'Give me deep feeling, *and* deep critical analysis, and make it happen all at the same time. The contradiction will be illuminating.'

In Chapter Three, the exercises discouraged mere *illustration* of the narration. Similarly, the exercises in this chapter encourage the actor to look for behaviours that *contradict* the implicit emotional tenor of a moment, giving expression to the tensions that arise from that opposition.

Exercise 32. *The Caucasian Chalk Circle*

Purpose: to seek ways to play emotion and commentary simultaneously.

Read this second exchange in Scene One between Grusha and Simon: the latter proposes marriage and the former accepts. This proposal scene happens within the mayhem of a violent and dangerous palace coup.

> SIMON. There you are at last, Grusha! What are you going to do?
>
> GRUSHA. Nothing. If the worst comes to the worst, I've a brother with a farm in the mountains. But what about you?
>
> SIMON. Don't worry about me. (*Polite again.*) Grusha Vachnadze, your desire to know my plans fills me with satisfaction. I've been ordered to accompany Madam Natella Abashvili as her guard.
>
> GRUSHA. But hasn't the Palace Guard mutinied?
>
> SIMON (*serious*). That they have.

GRUSHA. But isn't it dangerous to accompany the woman?

SIMON. In Tiflis they say: how can stabbing harm the knife?

GRUSHA. You're not a knife. You're a man, Simon Chachava. What has this woman to do with you?

SIMON. The woman has nothing to do with me. But I have my orders, and so I go.

GRUSHA. The soldier is a pig-headed man; he gets himself into danger for nothing – nothing at all.

(As she is called from the palace:)

Now I must go into the third courtyard. I'm in a hurry.

SIMON. As there's a hurry we oughtn't to quarrel. For a good quarrel one needs time. May I ask if the young lady still has parents?

GRUSHA. No, only a brother.

SIMON. As time is short – the second question would be: Is the young lady as healthy as a fish in water?

GRUSHA. Perhaps once in a while a pain in the right shoulder; but otherwise strong enough for any work. So far no one has complained.

SIMON. Everyone knows that. Even if it's Easter Sunday and there's the question who shall fetch the goose, then it's she. The third question is this: Is the young lady impatient? Does she want cherries in winter?

GRUSHA. Impatient, no. But if a man goes to war without any reason, and no message comes, that's bad.

SIMON. A message will come.

GRUSHA *is again called from the palace.*

And finally the main question…

GRUSHA. Simon Chachava, because I've got to go to the third courtyard and I'm in a hurry, the answer is 'Yes.'

SIMON (*very embarrassed*). Hurry, they say, is the wind that blows down the scaffolding. But they also say: the rich don't know what hurry is. – I come from…

GRUSHA. Kutsk.

SIMON. So the young lady has already made enquiries? Am healthy, have no dependants, earn ten piastres a month, as a paymaster twenty, and am asking honourably for your hand.

GRUSHA. Simon Chachava, that suits me.

SIMON (*taking from his neck a thin chain from which hangs a little cross*). This cross belonged to my mother, Grusha Vachnadze. The chain is silver. Please wear it.

GRUSHA. I thank you, Simon.

He fastens it round her neck.

SIMON. Now I must harness the horses. The young lady will understand that. It would be better for the young lady to go into the third courtyard. Otherwise there'll be trouble.

GRUSHA. Yes, Simon.

They stand together undecided.

SIMON. I'll just take the woman to the troops who've remained loyal. When the war's over, I'll come back in two weeks. Or three. I hope my intended won't get tired waiting for my return.

GRUSHA. Simon Chachava, I shall wait for you.[43]

The scene is often regarded as a charming love scene in which Simon is too embarrassed to woo or propose to Grusha, and so resorts to repeated formal questioning. Her assertiveness adds to the comic charm, especially when she agrees to marriage before he even proposes. While the scene is doubtless touching and the language has a sparse beauty, this reading ignores the scene's political substance and the function of its language. The political contradiction lies in the tension between human needs and the practical realities that this particular class faces:

- The characters represent the servant class.
- They frequently address each other in the third person.
- They focus on financial and practical considerations.
- Simon refers to these concerns as if he is making a series of bargaining offers.
- The scene occurs in a dangerous situation and where time is short.
- Simon uses ancient proverbs to describe these dangers.
- The language is almost completely free from romance.

Part 1. Revealing social realities

You are showing an audience an event that has already happened, so you can work on this scene as a demonstration of the above. A systematic way to approach this would be to run the extract several times, each time using one of the directions below:

- Deliver directly to the audience each line that relates to marriage as a business transaction.
- Deliver directly to the audience each line in which you refer to the other in the third person.
- Remember the characters have to negotiate the transaction carefully and in a hurry. This will mean that the tempo of some sections is urgent, or even rushed; in others it may seem as though the need for hurry has evaporated. These theatrical inconsistencies are useful ways of drawing an audience's attention to the contradictions of the scene.

- Remember the immediate danger they face. They have to be vigilant amid the violence of a palace coup; both are interrupting their duties to increasingly volatile employers. You can heighten this by increasing the physical distance between the figures and selecting moments when they look warily about them or move to evade danger.

Part 2. The exchanges in a negotiation

- After each question, such as 'May I ask if the young lady still has parents?', turn to the other actor to see as well as hear how the other character receives it.
- Add moments when the characters look at each other and make human contact. Look for both personal and circumstantial prompts in the situation that direct or interrupt moments of potential intimacy.
- As you work through the scene in this way, you will find that the characters – particularly Simon – play a series of distinct 'selves'. At one moment Simon is negotiating a deal, at another he is an embarrassed lover; at another a dutiful soldier asserting his manhood; at another a courteous man adhering to a traditional courtship ritual. At some moments he lives in spontaneous relation to Grusha; at others he appears to deliver commentary to a third person. The actor's job here is show the spectator each of these selves with *Gestic* clarity.

Parts 1 and 2 above will begin to reveal the tension between their emotional and practical needs.

Part 3. Looking at the scene in relation to the broader narrative

Read the section at the end of Scene Four in which they meet on opposite sides of a river. This happens several years later after he has spent this time as a soldier in the war. She admits she has now married someone else, but can't explain that she was tricked into a sham marriage. Simon sees a cap in the grass and assumes its owner is the love child of this marriage. She can't tell him that the child isn't hers – she may be overheard. He is bitterly heartbroken and turns to leave. She too is heartbroken, belatedly insisting the child isn't hers, only to contradict herself when soldiers appear, accusing her of kidnapping the child. He hears this and storms off.

Knowledge of what happens in this scene can help you to explore the emotional content of the proposal scene.

Part 4. Making decisions on what you want to show

Discuss the extent to which the proposal scene needs to reveal the personal feelings these characters have for each other. If the exchange is played with cold awareness of practical realities as implied by the commentary in Part 1 of this exercise, then Grusha's anguish and tears in the river scene will seem strange. This contradiction may be precisely the point you wish to make, implying that for Grusha, the marriage was solely a route to survival in a cruel world. The text says that there are tears in her eyes as she contemplates Simon's new paymaster living quarters. Are these the tears of a woman longing for security, or does she yearn for a home with a husband who loves her? Can she be heartbroken if the proposed marriage that was little more than a cold business deal?

Brecht reminds us that the actor should 'never forget it is the actor's duty to present living people'.[44] I would maintain that the contradiction of the proposal will only register if both sides of it are present: the audience need to see the characters' emotional need for intimacy *and* the economic and circumstantial realities that prevent it.

Part 5. Juxtaposing and integrating emotion with commentary

Now play the choices discussed in Part 4, modifying and refining as you go along.

Keep experimenting with physical manifestations to find the most effective way to draw an audience's attention to the contradictions in the scene, for example: a line concerning money could be delivered intimately, or the 'love token' gift of the cross could be taken by Grusha as a deposit that she knows will have to be redeemed later. The stage direction then says that he fastens it around her neck, which may look like romantic intimacy; it will seem strange if Grusha initially accepts it as part of a business deal.

Brecht gives them a powerful moment of indecision in which they stand together. Each may have an internal impulse to complete the event in some way: it may be with a touch or by taking one another's hands. They are aware that this would be *socially* 'inappropriate', while also sensing that walking away would be *emotionally* inappropriate. So they are left standing close to each other. You can decide how long they stand in this position and whether they look at each other. The moment can only communicate its human and political impact if both performers are emotionally 'full' at this point.

This approach is a good demonstration of Brecht's concept of realism, that is to say, behaviour influenced by social and economic realities. It acknowledges the importance of emotional and empathetic acting, but emotion is selected and arranged as part of a series of contradictions, conveying the plight of the servant class under particular circumstances.

Summary

The above exercise illustrates a dialectical relationship between feeling and commenting. The procedure can be summarised as follows:

Commentary

- Identify a scene's contradictions, social circumstances, social relations, power struggles.
- Consider the ways in which the scene resembles a transaction or negotiation – frequently a financial one.

Physical embodiment of commentary

- Establish clear physical manifestation of commentary, using past-tense narration, *Gestus* and *Haltung*; define special relationships.
- Consider the emotional impact on the characters of events in the whole play.
- Use emotion in juxtaposition or tension with commentary.

In this example from *The Caucasian Chalk Circle*, emotion is experienced and expressed by both characters in equal measure, with a 'rending contradiction' between empathy and demonstration expressed by each figure. Below is an example from the 'closet scene' from *Hamlet* (Act Three, Scene Four). I have already discussed the scene in Chapter Four, Part Two. In this way of working, emotion and reason are juxtaposed, one character releasing emotion, the other attempting control. A contradiction also exists in the tension between each character's bearing and what they say. Hamlet's arguments frequently seem intellectually faultless while the delivery has a desperate emotional energy; Gertrude scarcely has any arguments, and her responses could seem equally desperate, but the exercise requires the actor playing her to contain her emotions as much as possible. Gertrude's tensions and contradictions can reveal the social conditions that inform their choices of action. Hamlet's emotional extremes underline how ill-equipped he is to cope with the political realities at Elsinore.

Exercise 33. Reasons to Contain Emotion

Purpose: to use contradiction to control emotion and reveal social motivations.

Hamlet

This exercise using Act Three, Scene Four of *Hamlet*, requires the actor playing Gertrude to contain her feelings as much as possible, in contrast to Hamlet's near hysterical extremes. The point is to reveal a woman who makes decisions on the basis of the conditions in which she lives. At the outset she can be 'in denial' of any sensation of guilt, remaining convinced for long as possible that her position is justified and honourable. This reading can reveal a far more active woman than a weeping and largely passive recipient of Hamlet's castigation.

Gertrude's motivation can be interpreted as outlined in Exercise 30 in Chapter Four, Part Two. She knows Claudius's regime is totalitarian and ruthless, so marrying and remaining loyal to him is a viable survival strategy. Moreover, she was a member of a class-defined group of potential royal wives; once promoted to royalty, why should she relinquish that status? So if her husband dies, she must find a replacement to maintain her position.

1. Read the entire scene and divide it into significant events. The divisions can be marked by shifts in action, or by what the characters talk about.

2. Look at the moments immediately before or after the **numbers** inserted in the scene. Consider Gertrude's possible *Haltungen* at each of these moments (suggestions follow the extract).

Enter HAMLET.

HAMLET.

Now, mother, what's the matter?

QUEEN GERTRUDE.

Hamlet, thou hast thy father much offended.

HAMLET.

Mother, you have my father much offended.

QUEEN GERTRUDE.

Come, come, you answer with an idle tongue.

HAMLET.

Go, go, you question with a wicked tongue. **1**

QUEEN GERTRUDE.

Why, how now, Hamlet!

HAMLET.

What's the matter now?

QUEEN GERTRUDE.

Have you forgot me? **2**

HAMLET.

No, by the rood, not so:
You are the queen, your husband's brother's wife;
And – would it were not so! – you are my mother.

QUEEN GERTRUDE.

Nay, then, I'll set those to you that can speak. **3**

HAMLET.

Come, come, and sit you down; you shall not budge;
You go not till I set you up a glass
Where you may see the inmost part of you.

QUEEN GERTRUDE.

What wilt thou do? thou wilt not murder me?
Help, help, ho! **4**

LORD POLONIUS.

[*Behind.*] What, ho! help, help, help!

HAMLET.

[*Drawing.*] How now! a rat? Dead, for a ducat, dead!

Makes a pass through the arras.

LORD POLONIUS.

[*Behind.*] O, I am slain!

Falls and dies.

QUEEN GERTRUDE.

O me, what hast thou done?

HAMLET.

Nay, I know not:

Is it the king?

QUEEN GERTRUDE.

O, what a rash and bloody deed is this!

HAMLET.

A bloody deed! almost as bad, good mother,
As kill a king, and marry with his brother.

QUEEN GERTRUDE.

As kill a king! **5**

HAMLET.

Ay, lady, 'twas my word. **6**

Lifts up the arras and discovers POLONIUS.

Thou wretched, rash, intruding fool, farewell!
I took thee for thy better: take thy fortune;
Thou find'st to be too busy is some danger.
Leave wringing of your hands: peace! sit you down, **7**
And let me wring your heart; for so I shall,
If it be made of penetrable stuff,
If damned custom have not brass'd it so
That it is proof and bulwark against sense.

QUEEN GERTRUDE.

What have I done, that thou dar'st wag thy tongue 8
In noise so rude against me?

HAMLET.

Such an act
That blurs the grace and blush of modesty,
Calls virtue hypocrite, takes off the rose
From the fair forehead of an innocent love
And sets a blister there, makes marriage-vows
As false as dicers' oaths: O, such a deed
As from the body of contraction plucks
The very soul, and sweet religion makes
A rhapsody of words: heaven's face doth glow:
Yea, this solidity and compound mass,
With tristful visage, as against the doom,
Is thought-sick at the act. 9

QUEEN GERTRUDE.

Ay me, what act,
That roars so loud, and thunders in the index? 10

HAMLET.

Look here, upon this picture, and on this,
The counterfeit presentment of two brothers.
See, what a grace was seated on this brow;
Hyperion's curls; the front of Jove himself; 11
An eye like Mars, to threaten and command;
A station like the herald Mercury
New-lighted on a heaven-kissing hill;
A combination and a form indeed,
Where every god did seem to set his seal,
To give the world assurance of a man:
This was your husband. Look you now, what follows: 12
Here is your husband; like a mildew'd ear,

Blasting his wholesome brother. Have you eyes? 13
Could you on this fair mountain leave to feed,
And batten on this moor? Ha! have you eyes?
You cannot call it love; for at your age
The hey-day in the blood is tame, it's humble,
And waits upon the judgement: and what judgement
Would step from this to this? Sense, sure, you have,
Else could you not have motion; but sure, that sense
Is apoplex'd; for madness would not err,
Nor sense to ecstasy was ne'er so thrall'd
But it reserv'd some quantity of choice,
To serve in such a difference. What devil was't
That thus hath cozen'd you at hoodman-blind?
Eyes without feeling, feeling without sight,
Ears without hands or eyes, smelling sans all,
Or but a sickly part of one true sense
Could not so mope.
O shame! where is thy blush? Rebellious hell,
If thou canst mutine in a matron's bones,
To flaming youth let virtue be as wax,
And melt in her own fire: proclaim no shame
When the compulsive ardour gives the charge,
Since frost itself as actively doth burn
And reason panders will. 14

QUEEN GERTRUDE.

O Hamlet, speak no more:
Thou turn'st mine eyes into my very soul;
And there I see such black and grained spots
As will not leave their tinct.

HAMLET.

Nay, but to live
In the rank sweat of an enseamed bed,

Stew'd in corruption, honeying and making love
Over the nasty sty, –

QUEEN GERTRUDE.
O, speak to me no more;
These words, like daggers, enter in mine ears;
No more, sweet Hamlet!

HAMLET.
A murderer and a villain;
A slave that is not twentieth part the tithe
Of your precedent lord; a vice of kings;
A cutpurse of the empire and the rule,
That from a shelf the precious diadem stole,
And put it in his pocket!

QUEEN GERTRUDE.
No more!

HAMLET.
A king of shreds and patches, –

Some observations

- Gertrude's attitude at the beginning of the scene can be closed and cold: a woman convinced of her own innocence.
- She can be astonished at his initial impertinence.
- She can retain her self-possession as she calls for help, since he is the mad one and not she.
- She can be baffled by his reference to an act that 'roars and thunders'.
- She can regard his accusations as typical of a teenage boy, unable to accept his mother's choice of a second husband.

Suggested responses to numbered moments

1 Gertrude can enter with the *Haltung* of a divinely anointed monarch. She assumes that all subjects, including her son, will treat her with unquestioning subservience. She is astonished by his impertinence. Between moments 1 and 12, this way of seeing can be the strongest for Gertrude.

2 Her appearance is of an unassailable monarch upbraiding a subject whose impertinence is tantamount to treason.

3 Like all monarchs, she needs palace guards to keep her subjects in order.

4 While Hamlet's response is forceful and violent, Gertrude's self-possession can conquer her fear: a monarch is expected to be unflappable when faced with a hysterical son who some say is mad. Her line 'Thou wilt not murder me?' can either be played dismissively ('You can't kill me, I'm your Queen') or with steely control, as he may have threatened her with a weapon to stop her leaving. Her cry for help can be a call for a servant, rather than a yelp of desperation.

5 In her mind she had no notion of foul play in relation to the death of her former husband, so she can be genuinely astonished.

6 A stand-off: Hamlet has challenged her treasonously and she could accuse him, but he is her flesh and blood. He drags in the corpse before she can make her decision.

7 In his eyes, she is wringing her hands: for her, she is holding them tight in a *Gestus* of (attempted) self-control while in the presence of a madman who has just killed an innocent man.

8 Her demand is accusatory: *he* must explain his impertinence.

9, 10 She can listen to his speech with growing understanding: this boy is unable to cope with the loss of his father and with the simple reality of his mother remarrying. She may be unsettled by the roar and thunder of his accusation but her impulse can be to pity his innocence rather than condemn his disrespect. The extremes of his language can propel Hamlet close to hysteria while Gertrude remains in control. She can almost laugh affectionately at his naive rage.

11 Gertrude can be touched by Hamlet's deification of his father: but to Gertrude it shows Hamlet's failure to understand who his father really was. Her conflict is between sympathy and love for her innocent son and impatience with his inability to face reality.

12 Gertrude can convince herself that her son will learn to love Claudius when Hamlet gains the perspective that comes with maturity.

13 This is a much longer attack and is directed at Gertrude's judgement. Hamlet accuses her of having forsaken her reason – the very thing that Elizabethans held most dear and that which separates humans from animals. At what moment in this section does Gertrude's hard defiance break?

14, 15 Her cold resistance appears to be finally broken following his sustained accusation that she has lost her senses. Until now she believed she was justified, but now her conscience has overwhelmed her feudal morality.

His condemnation is intensified by the accusation that *her lust* is the cause of her loss of reason. An Elizabethan aristocrat can't ignore such an accusation of bestial degeneracy. She could tell him that her motive is strategic, but she knows this will disgust her son and put her in danger. She has, after all, just seen him thrust his rapier into the arras, thinking the man behind it was Claudius. So she can insert a '*Not… But…*' here – she did *not* admit her true motive, *but* instead begged him to be silent.

Each of moments 1–15 can be played as a defined *Gestic* attitude in resistance to deeply felt emotional impulses such as her love and pity for her son, her fear for her own safety, her deeply buried sense of guilt. Each might become manifest as a deliberate physical action, e.g. Gertrude holds her hands tightly in order to prevent herself from crying out in terror.

Death of a Salesman: Choreographing Emotion

Purpose: to reveal social realities by controlling emotional extremes.

This approach focuses on power relations, contradictions and contrasting perceptions of business. These are examined in relation to the protagonist's growing emotional trauma.

In Arthur Miller's play, Willy Loman is an ageing travelling salesman in New York and New England in the late 1940s. He has devoted his working life to a particular company, driving vast distances to sell merchandise. His income was made up of a basic salary plus commission, but now he is employed on commission only. His powers have waned with age, and his diminished alertness behind the wheel has made him a danger on the road. He has agreed with his wife to renegotiate his job with the company's young boss, Howard Wagner. In this scene, he visits Howard and makes several attempts to persuade him to take him off the road, even on a modest salary. By the end of the meeting, Howard tells the old man that the company no longer needs his services.

You will need to read the scene in full before working on the exercises. It comes a few pages in to Act Two of Miller's play. It can be anatomised as follows, broken down into events, their interpretation (what Brecht calls the *Fabel*), and implications for performance:

Event 1. Howard fixates on the tape recorder

Howard Wagner appears. He is absorbed in threading magnetic tape through a reel-to-reel tape recorder. He glances briefly at Loman as the latter appears, who calls to him with a 'pssst' sound.

Interpretation The event can be seen as a simple power transaction. Loman attempts to greet Howard as an equal, but Howard is fixated with his expensive, newfangled machine. In these moments, a 'power league table' can be seen as:

- Most powerful: the tape recorder.
- Second most powerful: Howard.
- Third most powerful: Willy Loman.

Practical notes: the Haltung *of Power* Howard's successive *Haltungen* can be that of a child, a boy in thrall to a new toy, and that of a man at ease in his own space. Loman's *Haltung* is of a man attempting ease and familiarity. When he is rebuffed, the actor can show Loman processing this by employing a '*Not... But...*': he could be on the point of giving in to his feelings of defeat, and then decide to continue with the exchange. The actor playing Loman can experiment with the extent to which he reveals the emotional cost these denials impose on the old man.

Event 2. Howard and his machine remind Loman that he is now excluded from the Wagner family

Howard enthuses about the machine, saying he has bought it for dictation but has used it for entertainment at home. He plays Loman recordings of his family and celebrates the cleverness and charm of his children's recordings. Loman attempts to share in Howard's enthusiasms but is ignored.

Interpretation For a company partner, a machine for work can become a toy for play. He can use company time and resources for private entertainment. This privilege is not available to an employee; Loman wants to talk business while Howard wants to play.

Practical notes: power relations expressed through use of space Loman attempts to maintain a familiar relationship between them, but Howard's interruptions and boasts about his children repeatedly wound Loman. The actor can play Loman's *resistance* to the hurt. These power relations are expressed through the characters' use of space: Loman might attempt to stride into the room but finds himself pushed to the edges; Howard dances around his machine, frequently turning his back on Loman. This staging can show how the old man is excluded from the trophies and privileges enjoyed by his young boss.

Event 3. Loman can't pay his insurance, so how can he afford a tape recorder?

Howard delightedly says the item costs 'only' a hundred and fifty dollars. The price is forty dollars more than the insurance premium that Loman can't afford but needs to pay. Loman says he will definitely buy this machine to catch up on radio programmes he misses while on the road. Howard asks him why he doesn't listen to the radio in the car. Loman asks, 'Whoever thinks of turning it on?'

Interpretation A consumer item reveals more economic and power differences, which Loman tries to ignore. He says he will buy a tape recorder for himself, but it's evidently an item that's well beyond his means; he attempts to shift the conversation to working as a travelling salesman. He knows he's been caught out by Howard's question about the radio in the car, because he can't afford one.

Practical notes: Positioning and the 'Not... But...' The machine can be positioned so that it seems like an object for worship, regarded with satisfaction by its owner and with longing and envy by those who can't have it. Rather than play the writhings of a desperate man, the actor playing Loman can resist each blow to his self-esteem, focusing on specifics, such as the hundred and fifty dollars, the recorder, and his failing attempt to control the conversation. His resistance can be explored in a series of '*Not... But...*' moments, in which we see both the defeat and Loman's denial of it. The actor can consider how these moments can be expressed through the rhythms of the character's breathing.

Event 4. Loman requests a job in town

Howard asks Loman why he isn't on the road, selling in Boston. Loman hesitates; Howard asks whether he has cracked up again. Loman says no, but he's decided not to travel any more. Howard asks what he will do instead. Loman reminds Howard that at the Christmas party Howard had promised him a job in town. Howard tells him he has no vacancies.

Interpretation Howard now faces a serious problem. Loman is a commodity of dwindling worth. If he 'cracked up', he's a liability to the firm; on the road Loman is only paid commission, so he costs the company very little; he will cost more in the office for little or no return. He knows a 'promise' made at a Christmas party is worth nothing. The action reveals their opposing perceptions of the company. Howard has a responsibility to keep it in profit and is faced with the reality of a completely unproductive worker. Loman sees the company in terms of past loyalties, promises, and sentimental attachments. He even claims to have had personal relations with Wagner Senior, who allegedly asked Loman what he thought of the name Howard for his newborn son.

The ensemble needs to decide whether these claims have some validity, in which case the play's subject is the changes to the business culture that have left Willy Loman behind. If they are fictional, they support the view that Loman has always naively sentimentalised the nature of business and is now a fantasist in his latter years. The latter view is reinforced if Howard responds to the story with a *Gestus* of pitying disbelief.

Practical notes: contradiction controls emotion Howard's *Haltung* is no longer that of a child, but an earnest, reasonable businessman: a gentle tone is needed to avoid a disruptive fuss in the workplace. The dissonance between his tone and his tough actions draws attention to the ruthlessness of company practice.

Loman's language is sentimental, but his verbal and physical *Haltung* can be that of a senior business executive approaching retirement. This draws attention to the contradiction between his delusions and the reality of his situation. The actor playing Loman can replace anguish with *astonishment* when told there isn't a job for him in town. An audience can be encouraged to be amazed that, despite his loyalty, the company won't look after him. Loman's 'performance' as 'the Great Magnate' continues to take its toll emotionally, and the performer experiments with the extent to which this is revealed, for example: Loman's actor could release his desperation at a moment when Howard's back is turned. Throughout he can explore a *Gestus* of astonishment.

Event 5. Legendary salesman was allegedly loved by his clients. Is this the American Dream? Is it a sentimental delusion?

In response to Howard's reminder that 'business is business' Loman tells Howard the story of David Singleman, the legendary salesman who, when aged eighty-four, could do business without leaving his hotel room and at whose funeral hundreds of buyers and fellow salesmen paid their respects.

Interpretation Loman's story lies at the heart of the play's politics. It holds up a vision of the American Dream for the audience to examine. It epitomises Loman's delusion.

Practical notes: holding up an argument for scrutiny Loman's language is rich with the musical cadences of nostalgic yearning. This is a pathetic aria of heroic desperation. The language is deeply affecting, and without a dialectical approach, the speech could so stir an audience's feelings of pathos that the politics are obscured. To counter this, the actors can work in the following way:

Loman's objective is to fight for his job and regain respect: put that aside for a moment and examine the Singleman story as an *argument* that's being held up to the audience for scrutiny.

a. *Loman's actor narrates the event* Preface everything by saying: 'These were Loman's strong arguments to prove he too was a great salesman.' As you continue, insert reminders that the speech is an argument: 'This is what he said to prove that selling is about being loved'; or: 'This is what he said when he demanded respect for selling.'

b. *Loman's actor delivers the speech as a CEO's address* The statements gain authority, particularly if this is a speech to junior staff. Self-pitying lines like: 'They don't know me any more' can be played with the *Gestus* of a boss rhetorically chastising his workers.

c. *The actors return to the text as written* The actor playing Loman can struggle to keep his desperation under control while retaining the discoveries in a and b. In this way, emotion should work in tension with that commentary.

Postscript

At the end of the speech, Howard is about to hurry off to 'see some people': while he plays this as a '*Not... But...*', Loman can release the emotion that he has kept at bay throughout when he tries to stop Howard from leaving.

Summary

The focus here is on physical externals: *Haltung*, *Gestus*, '*Not… But…*', contradiction, astonishment, both characters' relations to objects and their use of space. There is less emphasis on the characters' objectives. The purpose is to *show* the dynamics of this particular set of business transactions. Nevertheless, as the actors run through the scene after completing the above 'distancing exercises', they may need to be reminded of the scene's emotional undercurrent. As the ensemble observes the work, they can decide when Loman's emotional trauma can be revealed to support the political commentary.

The Actor and the Director respond to this treatment of Death of a Salesman.

ACTOR. All this seems to spell out meanings that an audience would get anyway.

DIRECTOR. You might be right, but in my experience, Miller's focus on a family in crisis means the audience respond emotionally to *them*, and pay little critical attention to the system he wants to criticise.

ACTOR. That is why the play has such power: it shows how the lives of ordinary people – people *we care deeply about* – are affected by the system.

DIRECTOR. I don't deny the audience should care about the characters. But we serve Miller's aims if we encourage them to look beyond the domestic situation.

ACTOR. Who is to say they won't?

DIRECTOR. In today's culture we fixate on individuals, not on the systems of social organisation that inform their behaviour.

ACTOR. If an audience wanted that, they would go to an evening class in sociology instead of the theatre.

DIRECTOR. But we can entertain *and* inform them with this approach. The problem with this play is that Loman is absurdly naive. An audience could blame him for his failures, and not criticise the system he operates in. Miller compensates for this by giving him language of such anguished lyricism that pathos can overwhelm everything. We can feel so sorry for Loman that we are blind to the mechanisms that the scene could reveal.

ACTOR. As I said, I think it would be all pretty plain to an audience.

DIRECTOR. All right, I can't convince you of that, but will you accept that the use of contradictory playing and the '*Not… But…*' offers a view that wouldn't be in a psychological rendering, namely that all this is not inevitable, that these characters *could do the opposite* of what they end up doing? That humans are essentially unstable and able to change? It is implicitly an optimistic take on a 'Modern Tragedy'.

ACTOR. Right. Miller is attempting to write a tragedy, and you are working against that with your interventions. You are actually undermining the play.

DIRECTOR. I think that is one of Brecht's major contributions. His methods breathe new life into old plays.*

ACTOR. I don't think that is something people want. You're cheating them of emotional engagement. They *want* to care and to be moved. And anyway, if you are moved, why shouldn't you want to change things?

* If the Director had done more research into Miller's work, he might have come up with a better reply here. On p. 194 of *Timebends* (London, Methuen 1987), Miller complained of the first performances of this play, saying 'there was too *much* identification with Willy, too much weeping… the play's ironies were being dimmed out by all this empathy.'

DIRECTOR. I don't think changing things is on an audience's mind as they wipe their tears away after seeing this play. I suspect that many of them want to be moved in the same way that you go to see a 'weepy' at the cinema. Can't we do better than turning emotions into commodities? Brecht is trying to put emotions to work so that they function as part of a contradiction. Why not try the exercises and see what they reveal?

ACTOR. Of course. I am open to possible ways of rethinking the scene. I am just wary of anything that's emotionally cold and propagandist.

DIRECTOR. That is something we can agree on.

The Actor implies that the above interpretations could be served by employing Stanislavskian methods. Indeed they could, and in several instances I have borrowed from the great man in this book. But for many, the *purpose* behind Stanislavsky's system is different. It is widely regarded as an effective way of generating 'truthful inner life' and ways of appearing *natural* when playing this inner life. Brecht's methods are designed to reveal underlying political processes *and to show them as unnatural, or constructed and thus changeable.* This 'showing' is explicit and provocative, with *Haltung* contradicting a character's natural impulses and making the moments intentionally jarring. So if we wish to focus on the way Howard's company operates, or examine Willy Loman's version of the American Dream, the behaviour the actors choose to do so might sometimes appear as the opposite of 'truthful' psychology.

Below is a series of exercises designed to help the performer develop an instinct for controlling and managing emotions in support of this attempt to open up sociopolitical mechanisms to an audience's scrutiny.

Exercise 34. Controlling and Manipulating Emotion

The Grieving Lover

1. Love lies bleeding An improvised speech in which a bereaved person grieves after discovering that their lover is dead. You will need to create a scenario and background in order to play the grief with authenticity. You are talking to a close friend.

2. It's a lie Repeat the scene using the same text: the speaker actually murdered their lover, so this time you have to perform the grief to the detectives in attendance.

3. It's a lesson Repeat the scene. The deceitful lover is a con artist, showing an apprentice how to con a detective, using the murder scenario as an example. The grief is performed and punctuated by verbal and non-verbal commentary delivered to the apprentice.

Elizabethan, Jacobean and Restoration comedies frequently feature deception scenes peppered with asides to co-conspirators onstage, or implicit partners in crime in the auditorium. What is the difference between the performed grief and the 'real' thing?

The Poker-Faced Conspirator

A conspirator discovers the corpse of a loved one, but mustn't cry out or they will give themselves away and endanger their own life. They meet the secret police and have to convince them they know nothing of the dead person. (A similar scenario appears in *Mother Courage and Her Children.*) This scenario can be worked on in three parts as above:

1. Imagine if the imaginary corpse was someone close to you. Work out the scenario and play the scene in a darkened space.

2. A workshop leader can send in the secret police: they must be briefed and prepared. They interrogate the conspirator.
3. Use above scenario 3 from The Grieving Lover, narrate and demonstrate what happened to a colleague or an apprentice.

A Declaration of Love

1. Establish the details and background for the scenario, and play the love declaration straight.
2. Play it as if it's all a con trick.
3. Alternate between honest protestation of love and 'asides' to an audience of friends in which you reveal your true dishonest self. This is a good exercise for playing emotional discontinuity with precision as you switch your emotional connection on and off.

A Marital Crisis in a Supermarket

1. The supermarket is virtually empty and no one is near you. Use this version to establish the nature and substance of the crisis. You may want to repeat this in order to discover more details in the relationship and the problem.
2. Continue the argument after noticing a friend of the family in the supermarket, first playing it as if you aren't sure if they've seen you, then as if you are sure they have.
3. Repeat, but now the person who has seen you is…
   - An official from social services.
   - A lawyer in a custody case.
   - Your boss from work or your partner's boss.

This is a good way of exploring the details of 'socially constructed' behaviour. Brecht's view was that all behaviour arises from social conditions and that people change radically in relation to the person they are with. The presence of different 'audiences' also emphasises the *performed* nature of social behaviour.

Conclusion

You will have seen that regulating and even choreographing emotion can sharpen political meanings, while enriching the theatrical experience a scene can offer. Far from draining a scene of its humanity, Brecht's approach increases it, deepening our understanding of how humans contend with the pressures and injustices of living. Portrayal of emotion can be seen as an essential part of a contradiction, rather than as an end in itself. Brecht challenges us to create theatre that promotes a complex way of seeing, illuminating scenes so that they are provocative and memorable.

You may also have noticed that the introduction of devices that manage emotion often gives the work a playful quality. Brecht considered this an essential element in rehearsal, and it is the focus of the next chapter.

Fun (*Spass*)

In England there is a longstanding fear that German art must be terribly heavy, slow, laborious and pedestrian. So our playing needs to be quick, light, strong. This is not a question of rushing, but of speed, not simply of quick playing, but of quick thinking. We must keep the tempo of a run-through and infect it with quiet strength, with our own fun.

Bertolt Brecht,
from a note pinned to the Berliner Ensemble noticeboard weeks before their tour to London in August 1956[45]

ACTOR. Well that's pretty astonishing...

DIRECTOR. What is?

ACTOR. All those references to lightness and fun. Everything we've done has been so *serious*. Brecht must have had a peculiar sense of humour.

DIRECTOR. Don't you think it's possible to approach his work playfully?

ACTOR. I haven't seen much evidence of that so far. His tone of voice is so *earnest*. He probably sat there reading out his favourite passages of Marx's *Das Kapital* saying: 'Oh this is just such FUN!'

DIRECTOR. But good productions of the plays are full of humour. One of his favourite words in rehearsal was *Spass,* which actually means 'fun'.

ACTOR. That certainly doesn't fit with what we've been doing.

DIRECTOR. Then let's try and work with the lightness he was talking about.

ACTOR. If you want to do that we will still have to work on the ideas. We can't just tack on a few silly games...

DIRECTOR. Right. We'll find a way of working on the theories *through* the playfulness, and not in spite of it.

Following are some non-text-based exercises for ensembles.

Exercise 35. 'Grandmother's Footsteps' with Variants

Purpose: to playfully developing awareness of groupings in space, and private and public Gestus.

It is vitally important that half the group observes while the other half performs variants of the game. The audience both learns from the watching and gives the performers a vital focus.

1. Standard This is a familiar children's game in which a group creeps up on the 'grandmother', whose back is turned. Those creeping up mustn't be seen to move when the grandmother turns. If the grandmother catches them moving, they are sent back to their starting point. The first person to reach and touch the grandmother becomes the grandmother in the next round.

2. With obstacles A chair and a table are placed between the group and the grandmother. Players must walk over the table and under the chair. Or vice versa. The arrangement of the obstacles increases the expansiveness of the participants' playground. Positioning one obstacle towards upstage-right and the other downstage-left expands the depth and breadth of the staging, enabling the group to create highly expressive tableaux.

3. With obstacles and with no grandmother The group must convince an audience that they are responding to a real grandmother even though one isn't present. The real grandmother can be reintroduced at any time to remind the group of how his/her presence influences their rhythms and shapes.

4. With eyes closed (both with and without a grandmother) Gradually, each group member is told to close their eyes (they can be blindfolded if the temptation to look is too great), so eventually the whole group plays blind. The level of tension within the group increases dramatically; they become acutely sensitive to the slightest sound, to each other's breathing and to the needs of the ensemble.

5. Innocent tableaux With their eyes open, the group has to perform a pose for the cameras when the grandmother turns around. It is as if they have been caught in a compromising position that they must cover up. The photographs can be named in advance: 'the ideal family', 'the innocent workforce', 'the undetected bank robbery', 'the innocent pickpockets', 'the Holy Order weren't dancing/drinking/having sex'.

A company of performers who play this game regularly will develop an awareness of the *Gestic* possibilities of each grouping while also fostering an ease and lightness in their work, and a shared delight in working as an ensemble.

Exercise 36. The Voice Orchestra

Purpose: to play with vocal ensemble Gests; *preparation for* Gestic *groupings exercise (see Chapter Four).*

A group of six to ten performers stand in a semicircle in front of a 'conductor'. The performers form groupings analogous to the sections of an orchestra. Each creates a vocal sound that is their interpretation of a particular attitude or *Gest*, for example: one can be scornful, one can be tragic, another heroic, another meditative, another impertinent, another lustful, another conspiratorial.

The conductor experiments with his/her orchestral palette and then creates a musical piece in which groups or individual 'musicians' are brought in and out. The conductor must find clear gestures to convey 'start', 'stop', louder', 'quieter', and other expressive qualities.

This exercise can be used to narrate the events of a scene in the form of a tone poem. To remind the ensemble of the events in a scene, the group can use words, each taking a short phrase at a time; to sensitise the group members to each other, the group can be asked to narrate a story. Here, the conductor starts and changes the speaker with increasing rapidity, producing ever-shortening phrases or half-phrases. Each narrator must complete the previous speaker's word or sentence.

In each version, the orchestral groupings can move into positions that best express their attitudes and their relationships to other groups. The ensemble members need to trust their instincts here: in the process they begin to discover possible *Gestic* groupings. This is good preparation for the groupings exercise in the *Gestus* chapter.

Playful *Verfremdung* Exercises

In this book I have tried to avoid exercises on *Verfremdung*, which means 'making the familiar strange', sometimes misleadingly translated as 'alienation'. The reason for this omission is that *Verfremdung* should be seen as an outcome of *all* the work. Nonetheless, it is still possible to train performers in maintaining a mindset that *never takes things for granted*, which is the essence of *Verfremdung*.

I mentioned the word 'alienation' above. This word has negative social, political and psychological connotations, and since the correct German word for 'alienation' is *Entfremdung*, I would advise the reader to avoid its use.

Exercise 37. Revisiting Objects

About twenty objects are spread out on the rehearsal-room floor. They might be, for example: a yoga mat, a T-shirt, a mobile phone, a cleaning cloth, a light bulb, an ironing board, a hammer, a frisbee, an old sock, a garden hose, an umbrella, a face towel, a tea towel, a chair.

1. Warming up the group's playfulness.

One at a time, each actor has to pick up an object, give it a name (not its real one) and explain what it does (not its real function), giving demonstrations where appropriate.

2. Using an object to defamiliarise aspects of contemporary life.

The workshop leader points to an object, says what it does (in italics below), and the performer demonstrates how it works, using some words to comment on or clarify the performance, and playing characters where appropriate.

- *This object shows how small logos sewn onto garments increase the happiness of the wearer.*
  The workshop leader points to a kitchen cloth/tea towel/old sock and asks a performer to show and tell us how this process works. The actor can demonstrate the wearer's attitudes before and after the logo is sewn on.
- *This object explains why gowns or robes make us respect those who wear them.*
  The object might be the T-shirt/yoga mat/towel.
  The workshop leader can call out: 'Show us the effects of the object in the State opening of Parliament/in the High Court/in the Vatican.' The absurd mismatch between a rubber mat and a grand costume, along with the actor's physical actions, encourage the viewer to question the dress codes and *Gestic* conventions of hierarchy.
- *This object enables the transfer of one footballer from one team to another for sums over ninety million pounds.*
  The object here could be a mobile phone, and the actor can play the role of footballer's agent, speaking to the player and representatives of the teams buying and selling. The actor can explore the *Gestus* of persuasion, ingratiation, hypocrisy, manipulation, charm, bullying, etc. To refine these physical statements, the actor can perform the demonstration in gobbledygook.
- *This object enables weight loss so rich people can look like underfed people from the developing world.*
  The object can be a garden hose and the two actors could demonstrate a liposuction procedure. Note that the satire may become disturbing, with references the horrors of famine. The company can then discuss the function of comedy when examining such realities.
- *This object is a piece of modern conceptual art valued at £6.5m pounds. Here's why it's worth every penny.*

The object can be an ironing board, and the performer can invent nonsensical justifications for its artistic and commercial value.

- *This object shows the benefits of a thermonuclear explosion and fallout, while showing how nuclear weapons protect us.*
  The object could be an umbrella, used to point to the devastation of nuclear war, and the nature of protection under the 'Nuclear Umbrella'.
- *These objects show the cathartic benefits of road rage.*
  The objects can be a chair and a frisbee. Once in the chair and behind a 'steering wheel', the actor is transformed into a driver negotiating the congested streets of a major city. Without the chair and disc there can be no rage.

The above exercises with objects may simply encourage a company of actors to have fun together, thereby building trust and ease in the rehearsal room. They may also foster playful subversiveness and an enthusiasm for exploring the expressive possibilities offered by objects. How a character uses an object is a comment on the character and on the object itself; using them playfully or even preposterously can sharpen an actor's awareness of their potential for creating meaning.

Following are some text-based exercises for smaller groups.

Exercise 38. Quick Tempo

Purpose: to help performers play with unforced lightness and pace.

Whenever actors run a play or scene at speed while making every effort to retain the detail of their work – as well as significant pauses and moments of stillness – they discover just how much excess baggage their work had been carrying hitherto. This increases their awareness of how much meaning can be conveyed per unit of time. The pauses gain tension, absurdities become more absurd and the work becomes more for the benefit of an audience and less for the performers. If they work at speed with a minimum of effort, the performance becomes a joy to watch. It's no surprise that Brecht refers so frequently to the importance of speed and lightness: by 'lightness' he meant 'ease'. This technique was often used at the Berliner Ensemble prior to the dress rehearsal.

Illegal Theatre

It can be enough for actors simply to play a scene at pace and to be reminded to work without tension and strain. But if they are given a reason for doing so, it might open the work to interpretative possibilities.

1. *Play the scene as if its content is illegal* The secret police are next door. Attempt to convey all the information in the scene before they come in.
2. *Play the above, but silently* Everything has to be fast, clear and silent, particularly the actors' feet.
3. *Showing how it's done* Play the 'illegal' version, but as if the performers are instructing a novice: it's a demonstration, so there are no police next door. In this position of safety, the version can be played with almost nonchalant ease.

Using Time Limits and Music

If a scene is about two minutes long, the actors can be asked to retain its 'truth' and detail while performing it in no more than sixty seconds. In a variant of this, the scene is accompanied by a piece of music of that length. The performers must finish the scene as the music ends. Below are some musical suggestions for scenes of various lengths. In general actors can be asked to reduce the normal length of a scene by about forty per cent.

- The performers should allow the emotional character of the music to influence the way they play the scene.
- Performers should think of the music as representative of their inner life or the rhythms of the story, but they should avoid dancing or grooving to the music.
- They can also do their best to *resist* the influence of the music: it will still influence them, despite their best efforts.

Lasting 1 minute: Chopin's 'Prelude B flat minor, Op. 28 No. 16', marked '*presto con fuoco*' (fast and with fire). A tempestuous piece of virtuoso piano played at a furious tempo.

Lasting 1 minute 30 seconds: Haydn's 'String Quartet Op. 9 No. 6' fourth movement, marked '*presto*'. A lighter, more playful piece.

Lasting 2 minutes 10 seconds: Haydn's 'String Quartet in D major, Op. 64 No. 5, "The Lark"'. Fourth movement (with a false ending a few seconds before it actually ends). Actors can be encouraged to develop physical energies and shapes in keeping with the lightness and playfulness of this piece.

Lasting 3 minutes: Scarlatti's 'Sonata in D minor Kk 517'. Pieter-Jan Belder's harpsichord recording has relentless drive and the sound of the harpsichord has a mechanical quality. The piece is in four sections of about forty-five seconds each. This could be useful for a scene that is divided in this way – or indeed this structure may enable performers to discover unexpected narrative shifts in the scene.

Exercise 39. Sit–Stand–Lie

Purpose: to develop playfulness in the ensemble; revisiting contradiction and power relations.

1. *Original version* Groups of three. Each member of the group of three takes up a different position, for example: A can sit, B can stand, C can lie. Then, without being prompted, all three must change their position, and no position can ever be taken by two people. The group can vary the speed, rhythm or movement quality of each change.
2. *First variation* The workshop leader can play a range of musical extracts in a range of styles, and the *Gestic* relationships in each trio can change with each musical change. The workshop leader can ask the whole ensemble to move together, incorporating sustained moments of stillness.
3. *Second variation* The combination of positions is used when working on a scripted scene involving three people (see suggested scenes below). The actors will need to know the scene quite well before using this exercise.

   The physical positions can reveal power relationships, sometimes illustrating the dynamics in the writing, while on other occasions offering a challenge to the scene's apparent power hierarchy. The company can discuss how the movements illuminated the power shifts in the scene. Was something unexpected revealed?
4. *Third variation* First working without text, the positions can now become more explicitly expressive of power or status relations:
   - In preparation for a three-person scene: sit–stand–bow.
   - In preparation for a four-person scene:
     sit–stand–bow–kneel.

- In preparation for a five-person scene: sit–stand–bow–kneel–lie prostrate.
- In preparation for a six-person scene: lounge–sit–stand–bow–kneel–lie prostrate.

Once the performers have developed a strong connection with each other working off-text, a scene can be introduced. A change in position should come from a narrative shift in the scene or a character's change of thought. Each performer should be encouraged to be surprised by and respond to each other's changes. In larger scenes, performers may have to be sparing with changes or the scene will dissolve into chaos. In each case actors can become aware of the game's *Gestic* and comic possibilities.

Suggested scenes for three actors

- Brecht's *The Caucasian Chalk Circle*, Scene Four: Azdak, Shauva and the Fugitive Duke.
- Shakespeare's *Twelfth Night*, Act One, Scene Five: Viola, Olivia and Maria.
- Shakespeare's *The Merchant of Venice*, Act One, Scene Three: Shylock, Antonio and Bassanio.
- Shakespeare's *Hamlet*, Act Two, Scene Two: Hamlet, Rosencrantz and Guildenstern.

Suggested scenes for four actors

- Eugène Ionesco's *The Bald Prima Donna*, scenes with the Smiths and the Martins.

Suggested scenes for larger casts

- Brecht's *The Caucasian Chalk Circle*, any of the trial scenes.
- Howard Barker's *Victory*, the bank interlude.
- Chekhov's *Uncle Vanya*, Act Three, immediately from Serebyakov's announcement that he is going to sell the estate.
- Maxim Gorky's *Philistines*, Act Four.

Exercise 40. Missiles

Purpose: to playfully focus language, power struggles and alliances in a scene.

In the sentences following the quotation that introduces this chapter, Brecht suggests that lines can be tossed between actors like 'so many tennis balls'. Throwing a physical object at the person to whom a line is directed can remind an actor of where the stress lies in a sentence and of the need for words to hit their target.

In this exercise, a range of missiles can be used: wet sponges or balls of paper have enough weight, they don't hurt the target, and a direct hit gives great satisfaction to the thrower.

Each player has an arsenal of projectiles; they can only throw them when they are speaking; they throw them at the person whom they are addressing – or at the person they wish to attack when they are speaking; they *must* throw on the operative word in each sentence.

This exercise has been particularly useful when working with drama-school students on *Celebration* by Harold Pinter. In a restaurant, brothers Lambert and Matt sit at one table with their trophy wives – who happen to be sisters. Sinister and vulgar, these men describe themselves as 'strategy consultants'. Lambert explains that this means that they don't carry guns. At a quieter table sit Russell and Suki.

In the exercise, each actor was armed with a bowl of grapes. The exercise revealed the intricacies of the power struggles both within the larger group and between that larger table and the other.

As with all the exercises in this book, the point is to discover how to make this work for yourself, but I will give a very short extract, with suggested operative (throw) words in bold (all bold text is mine):

MATT (*to* RUSSELL). You're a **banker**? Right?

RUSSELL. That's right.

MATT (*to* LAMBERT). He's a **banker**.

LAMBERT. With a big **future** before him.

MATT. Well, that's what **he** reckons.

LAMBERT. I want to ask you a **question**. How did you know he was a **banker**?

MATT. Well, it's the way he **holds** himself, isn't it?[46]

The missile need not be thrown hard; the physical quality of throw will inform the vocal quality of textual delivery. In most cases, the brothers direct their missiles at Russell even when they speak to each other.

These exercises are designed for smaller groups, but they work effectively if the rest of the ensemble observes. The group can use the feedback to develop the ideas.

Exercise 41. Playing with Contradiction

Purpose: to playfully increase the performer's bravery and willingness to work beyond the psychological; using contradiction to reveal possible meanings; playing contradictions with definition.

Intelligent Stupid

A performer presents the explanation given below. S/he must know and understand it as well as possible in advance. The performer must present the explanation as if it is in his/her words; the workshop leader calls out 'Intelligent!' or 'Stupid!' and the performer must change immediately from each of these attitudes/characteristics without changing the text. The task here is to discover ways of representing the struggles of a dull mind when expressing highly sophisticated and complex ideas. It may come from baffled or quizzical *Gests*.

> In Einstein's theory of general relativity he proposed that massive objects cause a distortion in space-time. This is experienced as gravity. We know that Sir Isaac Newton said that the strength of the gravitational force between two objects is determined by the mass of each object and the distance between them.
>
> We also know that in his theory of special relativity, Einstein demonstrated that the speed of light within a vacuum is always the same: it doesn't matter if the person looking at it is going fast or slow; light always travels at the same speed. This led him to the theory that space and time were bound together: he called this 'space-time'. So if two observers were in different positions in space-time, two events taking place at the same time for one observer would appear to take place at different times for another observer…

In successive versions, the prompter can signal a change with a clap or a bell; after that the performer can play the contradictions without being prompted. In each case, it is useful to ask members of the ensemble to watch and comment. What meanings did the contradictory shifts give to the presentation?

Courageous Cowardly

1.

Performers explore how courage and cowardice are expressed in terms of physical rhythms, shapes, and breath patterns. These *Gests* are best explored while engaged in an activity (e.g. sweeping the floor, arranging chairs, painting a wall, ordering a drink, waving to a crowd). This is essentially the same as the familiar parlour game 'In the Manner of the Word'.

Performers can give themselves an imaginary visual stimulus that provokes a cowardly or courageous physical response.

2.

As the performers are engaged with a specific activity, the workshop leader calls out 'Cowardly!' or 'Courageous!' If the performer struggles with these calls, the leader can call out: 'An axe murderer is coming towards you!' or: 'Draw your weapon and face the murderer!' The performers must transition seamlessly and with precision.

3.

A performer alternates between courage and cowardice when delivering the following piece of heroic text from Shakespeare's *Henry V*, Act Four, Scene Three. At each change of thought, marked by a bold forward slash in the text below, the workshop leader calls either of these *Gests*, as in part 2. It is helpful for the person calling to request a change on each mark. Everyone needs to get to know the material before attempting the exercise.

He which hath no stomach to this fight,
Let him depart; his passport shall be made
And crowns for convoy put into his purse /
We would not die in that man's company
That fears his fellowship to die with us /
This day is call'd the feast of Crispian
He that outlives this day, and comes safe home,
Will stand a tip-toe when this day is nam'd,
And rouse him at the name of Crispian /
He that shall live this day, and see old age,
Will yearly on the vigil feast his neighbours,
And say 'To-morrow is Saint Crispian.' /
Then will he strip his sleeve and show his scars,
And say 'These wounds I had on Crispian's day.' /
Old men forget; yet all shall be forgot,
But he'll remember, with advantages,
What feats he did that day. Then shall our names,
Familiar in his mouth as household words –
Harry the King, Bedford and Exeter,
Warwick and Talbot, Salisbury and Gloucester –
Be in their flowing cups freshly rememb'red. /
This story shall the good man teach his son;
And Crispin Crispian shall ne'er go by,
From this day to the ending of the world,
But we in it shall be remembered /
We few, we happy few, we band of brothers
For he today that sheds his blood with me
Shall be my brother be he ne'er so vile,
This day shall gentle his condition; /
And gentlemen in England now a-bed
Shall think themselves accurs'd they were not here,
And hold their manhoods cheap whiles any speaks
That fought with us upon Saint Crispin's day.

This can be attempted several times: initially, a stimulus to a cowardly response could make the speaker look as if they have seen a ghost or monstrous apparition. The mismatch with the heroic text will seem absurd or even grotesque. With repeated attempts, the stimulus provoking cowardice can become more subtle. The performer can internalise it, and we see a young new leader struggling with his doubts and fears.

Ruthless Compassionate

The boss dismisses an employee.

1. The dismissal

A pair rehearses a simple scenario in which the boss explains to the employee why s /he has to sack them. The workshop leader records the content.

2. The boss's changing behaviour

The text of the original version is accurately replayed while the workshop leader calls 'Ruthless!' or 'Compassionate!' with each change of thought. As with many of these exercises, performers have to play actions without knowing precisely what motivated them (this is often described as working 'outside-in'). The group can discuss whether the boss's changes seemed credible, and compare them with…

3. The boss's changing motivations

The workshop leader calls out prompts to the boss, such as: 'This employee lost the firm thousands of pounds'; 'S/he has a partner and has to support three children'; 'S/he is divisive and is a threat to you'; 'His/her house will be repossessed'. It is essential to accurately replay the dialogue rehearsed in part 1, and so this will demand *Gestic* precision, since intentions will have to be conveyed physically while the text remains unchanged.

4. The employee's responses

The focus is now on the employee's contradictory impulses. The workshop leader calls either 'Submissive!' or 'Defiant!' to the actor playing the employee. Here, the prompter imposes the impulses on the scene, and the actor has to make sense of them, turning them into responses to the boss's shifts in manner or tactics. Afterwards, observers can tell the performers what meanings were communicated by the stark changes in the employee's responses.

5. Without the prompter

The above impositions forced the performers to play extreme changes. This should have stretched the actors, allowing them to embody contradiction with bravery. They can now play the shifts without the prompter. They don't have to worry about the psychological 'truth' or plausibility of their responses: they simply follow the instincts they have developed from the previous phases of the exercises. Afterwards, the spectators comment on the meanings or 'truths' that they revealed.

This exercise is similar to those in which actors explore the emotional 'push and pull' of a scene. The difference here is that the prompts come from outside the scene and they have to be played regardless of whether the actor had the initial impulse to do so. This can push the performer to extend choices beyond his or her comfort zone.

Exercise 42. Playing with Musical Mismatches

Kurt Weill composed a smoky and seductive tango for Brecht's 'Ballad of Immoral Earnings' in *The Threepenny Opera*. The lyrics describe sexual violence and a backstreet abortion, which ends with the foetus being flushed down the sewer. The mismatch of harrowing words and sensual music draws attention to the horror of the story. It's likely that the lyrics become memorable and provoke discomfort among the audience. As the characters sing with erotic nostalgia, an audience might repeatedly ask themselves, 'Did they *really* say that?' This is *Verfremdung* in action, and in our un-shockable times it is a useful way of sharpening the impact of shocking material.

Playing with deliberate mismatches between music and content can produce moments of striking *Verfremdung*, while liberating comedy or unexpected meanings in a scene.

Example: comic music accompanies high drama

Chekhov is said to have complained that Stanislavsky's productions missed the comedy in his great plays, and indeed the comic absurdity of many scenes in Chekhov's four masterpieces is often what makes them so heartbreaking. In this exercise, the actors alternate between accepting *and* resisting the comic energy of the music as they play the scene. No matter how hard they try to resist the music, its presence will make them aware how preposterous their characters can seem, for example: Act Three of *Uncle Vanya* with 'Sweet Georgia Brown' by the Rosenberg Trio, or 'Reinventing the Wheel' by Orkestra del Sol.

Other mismatches that can be attempted both with script and improvised material:

- Soothing music and adrenalised action ('Where We Used to Live' by Esbjörn Svensson Trio).

- Banal music and human atrocity ('Falling' by Ant and Dec).
- Heroic music and banal action ('Ride of the Valkyries' by Wagner).
- Trivial music and self-important action ('Buzz Buzz Buzz' by Jonathan Richman and the Modern Lovers).

In each case, a group of observers can comment on the new meanings that are suggested by these deliberate mismatches. This process can contribute to the group's ideas for the way the scene or whole play is staged.

Exercise 43. Discovering Status

Purpose: to see power relations and characters in a new way.

Actors are usually familiar with status exercises, but for more details see the *Gestus* exercise on status energies in Chapter Four (page 17). In these exercises, performers are given playing cards to denote their status. Use only the cards from ace to ten, with ace representing ultra-low status and ten the highest. The game is based on the principle that a higher status person will take up the most space, commanding an invisible bubble around them that lower status people will not dare to invade. Conversely, the lowest status person will occupy so little space that they will seem invisible. With no malicious intent, a higher status person will look and walk 'through' the space occupied by a person of low status.

Discovering a Character's Status

Each player is given a playing card, and they must not look at it. They hold it in front of them so it's visible to their fellow players. The entire group walks around the studio. It can be useful for each player to give themselves a series of points as destinations and attempt to walk to each point. They will discover their status by noticing how the other players treat them as they attempt to reach their destination: some may make way for them, while others might walk across their path as if they don't exist. It's easy to identify as an ace or a ten; much harder to differentiate between a five and a six. The more that players practise, the more accurate they will become. Once it seems that the players have a good idea of their status, the workshop leader can call a 'line-up', with highest status players at one end of the line and lowest at the other.

Discovering Your Status in a Scene

Once actors have become skilled in the above, the principle can be applied to scene work. It is advisable to start with a two-hander scene in which each character's status seems clear from the text. Remember *neither actor must see their own status card*: they discover it through the scene. The workshop leader gives a playing card that best represents each performer's status. In all cases, this exercise is useful once the actors feel that they know the scene well. It forces each actor to focus on their scene partner, making the exchange full of heightened energy. Here are a few examples:

Harold Pinter, The Hothouse, *Act One, Scene One*

Extract from the point when Roote asks whether there has been a death on the premises, to Gibbs' announcement that it's Christmas Day.

Roote runs a sinister institution for inmates whose reason for incarceration isn't clear; he is losing his grip. Gibbs seems deferential towards his boss.

- First version: Roote is given a 7 playing card, and Gibbs a 4. The cards will force Gibbs to be deferential, but the text makes him intangibly insubordinate: Gibbs can discover power through subservience.

- Second version: both are given 7. Gibbs' increased confidence can help to intensify Roote's paranoia.

Continue to experiment with different combinations, observing the meanings that they bring out of the scene.

Howard Barker, Victory, *Act Two, Scene One*

Charles I has returned as the monarchy is restored. Bradshaw, the widow of an executed Parliamentarian, wishes to transform her life by travelling like a vagabond to London to recover his body. In this scene, she meets Charles's spurned lover Devonshire on an estuary beach. Devonshire is a victim of the cruelties of court gossip, ill-treatment by men, and the agonies of seven miscarriages. Both women are externally assertive but deeply vulnerable.

- First version: both are given an 8 playing card.
- Second version: Bradshaw 8 and Devonshire 3.
- Third version: both 8 again, incorporating the discoveries made in the first two versions.

Simon Stephens, Country Music, *Act Two*

Matty visits his elder brother Jamie in prison. Jamie was convicted for killing a notorious child abuser who had threatened his younger brother. Jamie's life appears to be in ruins and his brother feels intense guilt for visiting now: he has put it off for a long time, and he is there now to tell his brother that Jamie's ex-partner and mother of his child has left town with another man.

- First version: Jamie 5 and Matty 3.
- Second version: Jamie 9 and Matty 8.

Discuss what was discovered and choose cards accordingly for subsequent versions.

Shakespeare, Measure for Measure, *Act Two, Scene Four*

This immensely complex scene would benefit from this exercise only once the actors have understood the convolutions of its religious arguments. Angelo's language is so contorted that Isabella fails to understand his intentions until he spells them out when he says: 'Believe me on mine honour / My words express my purpose.'

- Angelo gets a 9, and Isabella a 7. Angelo's high card will mean that Isabella's behaviour towards him will confer on him the semi-divine status of 'the voice of (religious) law', which is how she sees him. While her status card is lower than his, 7 is unexpectedly high for a novice nun visiting the most powerful man in the dukedom. It is unlikely to give her greater power, but it may increase Angelo's self-hatred: the guilty man thinks that she must suspect him, since his crime is so apparent to himself.

As before, it is important for the company to discuss their observations from the above, informing the choice of different cards for subsequent versions.

Shakespeare, Macbeth, *Act Two, Scene One*

The exchange between Banquo and Macbeth. The scene is rich with tension: Banquo may faintly suspect Macbeth; the latter may sense he is under suspicion; Macbeth is possessed with the thought of a murder that relentlessly approaches, battling his guilt and fear.

- Macbeth gets a 7, Banquo a 10. This allocation anticipates the way Macbeth feels intimidated by Banquo's regal bearing, as the former explains in the speech in Act Three, Scene One, beginning 'To be thus is nothing, but to be safely thus'.

Two observations

It might seem that using a card denoting a fixed status runs counter to Brecht's assertion that the human personality is unstable, inconsistent and subject to change as conditions change. This would apply if the players saw their card in advance, and then 'performed' its status as they rehearsed the scene. But here the performers are in a constant state of investigation and discovery: each tries to work out their status based on the actions of the other character, and this occurs in interaction with the events and lines in the text itself. This gives the exercises dynamic instability, in keeping with Brecht's conception of human relations.

Secondly, all the above exercises require actors and director to engage in a process of shared experimentation. They observe the possible meanings that arise from possible choices, discuss them, and experiment further to find choices that most effectively articulate a play's social meaning. This is described as an 'inductive' method in Brecht's 1941 essay 'On the Gradual Approach to the Study and Construction of the Figure'[47] and is explained with elegant clarity by David Barnett in his book *Brecht in Practice*.[48] It is the opposite of a process in which either the director imposes a 'concept' on a play, or an actor imposes a preconceived notion of the character.

Discovering and Playing the Wrong Status

As anticipated, players can be given a card representing the 'wrong' status. At moments the scene might become absurd – particularly if a king is treated with contempt and a servant with deference. But in the process, performers can discover unexpected meanings as expected power relations are 'made strange'.

Note: comparable discoveries can be made when applied to Jacques Lecoq's Levels of Tension: these states of energy are beautifully described in John Wright's book *Why Is That So Funny?*[49] The exercises increase physical eloquence and precision, while deliberately applying the wrong state of tension to a scene, and can reveal contradictory or unexpected elements of a character's make-up.

Conclusion

It has become a commonplace for practitioners to proclaim the value and importance of playfulness in the rehearsal room. In these exercises, the playful element isn't sought for its own sake: they are an attempt to put the fun to work, pulling the performer's attention (and anxiety) away from him/herself, promoting Brecht's preference for 'showing', and opening up inductive ways of interpreting a scene or character. The element of play can give an overly earnest or self-critical actor permission to play physical or vocal extremes without worrying about getting the scene 'right'.

Final Thoughts

The best way to use this book is to improve on it. Keep playing with the exercises: they function best as part of a continuous process of adaptation and development, promoting both complexity and clarity, and most importantly, reminding you that performance is for an audience.

A dialectical approach to theatre provokes an audience into considering *why* significant events take place: Marxism may have lost political credibility in these postmodern times, but Brecht's demand that we need not accept events as inevitable and irredeemable is a valid and inspiring task for any artist. I hope these exercises will enrich both your practice and your view of humanity.

Theory is not the same as practice. Theory is simply the provocation, and practice is messy, protean, sometimes bewildering, and frequently exciting. You will improve on this book by experimenting and testing its propositions, producing work that bears your individual stamp, making new discoveries as you respond to the political or cultural realities that surround you.

Glossary

Brechtian

This term is usually used to describe a piece of theatre that employs staging devices associated with Brecht's own productions. The received view of such devices is that they are used to draw attention to the artifice of the play, preventing an audience from becoming 'hypnotised' by the dramatic illusion. Indeed, Brecht's challenge to the physical structure of the bourgeois theatre of the 1920s was radical and political. Out went the orchestra pit and proscenium arch separating the action from the spectators. Brecht's friend and interpreter Walter Benjamin described this as a 'magic circle',[50] which Brecht replaced with a public platform, incorporating placards or projections designed to frame or comment on the action. While this made a significant impact in the late 1920s, such radicalism is often lost on today's audiences, who are used to seeing theatre in a vast range of non-theatre settings, frequently with sophisticated audio-visual devices. More significantly, many of the aesthetic devices listed above disappeared from Brecht's postwar work at the Berliner Ensemble.

Another problem with the above definition is that it informs descriptions of productions that employ the devices *without the purpose Brecht originally intended for them*. These devices were a part of his early attempts to present events in an unfamiliar way and they relate to the short period from 1926 to the middle of the next decade.

I would therefore suggest that the term 'Brechtian' is best used to describe political intentions and approaches to understanding plays, rather than aesthetic devices. It is a type of theatre that proposes that human actions have social and historical causes. It focuses on events or situations rather than on individual characters. It draws attention to the social context for these events, revealing contradictions in the characters' actions, leading to decisions and change. It invites an audience to regard what they see as contingent on particular conditions, with the implication that if the conditions changed, humans would change with them.

Dialectics

A clash of opposites leading to change within an individual or ultimately to society. Brecht's practice actively seeks out opposites and orchestrates their opposition. The '*Not... But...*' technique described in Chapter Two indicates both what the character chooses to do and what they choose *not* to do. The violent 'tussle' between emotion and commentary referred to in Chapter Five is a powerful example of dialectical theatre in action. A character's contradictions embody incompatible impulses, leading to profound instability and the potential for transformation. Brecht also uses the term 'materialist dialectic'. The word 'materialist' indicates a rejection of the presence of fate or divine agency in human affairs. For Brecht, the reality informing the action of his plays is the *material conditions* in which the characters live.

Empathy

For Brecht, this was the process in which the actor convinces the spectator that s/he has emotionally placed him/herself 'in the shoes' of their character, leading to an analogous feeling of emotional identification between spectator and character/performer. Brecht was sceptical of empathy, possibly because he associated it with the emotional manipulation employed by the Nazis. His scepticism may also have come from a conviction that it could lead actors to 'identify' with their characters so much that they would say they 'were' Grusha or Mother Courage: for him this would fatally miss the point that these were characters in a *story* and were demonstrating actions that were particular to specific historical situations (see Chapter Five). Scepticism of an actor's empathy is central to his conception of theatre. If empathy means that the actor completely identifies with their character, s/he will bring his or her contemporary understanding of humans to the role. But if we accept that relationships between, say, men and women have varied a great deal over time, then Brecht argues that actors should see their characters more critically, placing them in their historical context.

Epic Theatre

The word 'epic' is derived from the literary term describing ancient extended narrative works by poets such as Homer and Virgil. In his version of Epic Theatre, developed from 1926, Brecht proposed a comparable episodic structure, selecting key events in an expansive historical chronicle. The expansiveness of Shakespeare's plots and landscapes anticipate Brecht's version of this narrative structure (see Narrative below). While Shakespeare's plays can be divided into five acts (even if he didn't do so himself), Brecht deliberately attempts to separate each episode. The clearest example of this is *Mother Courage and Her Children*, in which scenes are presented in the context of significant historical events, demonstrating a causal relationship between human action and prevailing social conditions. Brecht also used the term Epic Theatre to describe staging conventions and techniques that would offer a Marxist (see below) perspective on human relations, by setting them at a distance.

Fabel

A politically engaged interpretation of a scene's story, that actively seeks out contradictions and accounts for them. It is based on a belief that drama can expose inequalities and injustices, proposing ways to change the system that causes them.

Gestus

An actor's physicality that places a character in a social context. Brecht uses the term when discussing the physical manifestation of a social attitude, position or standpoint, but these are more accurately examples of the term *Haltung* (see below). *Gestus* is most helpfully seen as a demonstration a character's social position. This is frequently referred to as the *Social Gest*(*us*) in which the performer selects physical shapes, movements and actions reveal a character's social position, demonstrating how behaviour is socially conditioned (see Chapter Four).

Haltung

A key component of *Gestus*: the frequently changing postures or physical gestures that express a character's attitude as they respond to something. *Haltungen* (plural form) change as a character reacts to the changing social world around them (see Chapter Four).

Historicised action, Historicisation

Presenting events in a play as moments in history, viewed through the lens of the present, enabling the viewer to rethink the present by contemplating the past. This can involve observing how things have changed, thus encouraging further transformations; equally, it can involve observing how certain injustices or social relations have prevailed, encouraging an audience to challenge and reform them (see Chapter 3). Historicisation is achieved when the director and ensemble engage in rigorous research into a play's period and place. By then applying practical approaches such as the '*Not... But...*' and *Gestus*, performers can expose the 'strangeness' of these historical social attitudes and conventions.

Marxism

While Brecht was profoundly influenced by his readings of Marx from 1926 onwards, he rarely mentioned him by name. He was particularly attracted to Marxist Dialectics, which propose that irreconcilable social conflicts arise from the inequalities in any given society. These conflicts – between the elites that control production and those they employ to deliver it, or between elites and newly emerging social groups – become intractable and lead to powerful social ruptures or revolutions, which in turn produce new systems of production.

Montage

An often discontinuous series of images or events that are organised so as to encourage the spectator to construct connections between them and/or to question received attitudes.

Narrative

For my purposes, I use the term to mean storytelling theatre, in which events are presented at having already taken place, involving a narrator or devices that serve a storytelling function. Epic Theatre creates a tension between what an audience is told and what they are shown. Nowadays, this practice is so familiar that Epic Theatre has questionable utility, and it seems that Brecht anticipated this in his later years, replacing it with 'dialectical theatre'.

'Not... But...'

The portrayal of a character's moment of decision, in which the actor reveals what they *didn't* do as they enact the choice dictated by the script (see Chapter Two). This technique reveals the inherent contradictions in human actions, while demonstrating that actions are not inevitable, but are the result of conscious human choice.

Spass

German for 'fun'. For Brecht this was an essential ingredient in the rehearsal room (see Chapter Six).

Verfremdung

This word is frequently unhelpfully translated as 'alienation' (*Entfremdung* is the German word for this, and is used by Marx to describe how the exploited worker is *alienated* from his or her humanity. This process has nothing to do with *Verfremdung*, so translating that word as 'alienation' only confuses matters). *Verfremdung* is usefully translated as 'making familiar things appear strange'. Brecht wants practitioners and spectators to avoid taking what they see for granted, which would lead them to accept dramatic events as inevitable. While the staging devices associated with 'Brechtian Theatre' supposedly further this end, I would suggest that *Verfremdung* occurs when a moment of action enables the viewer to see a character or a social phenomenon from a new and/or unexpected perspective. *Verfremdung* is not a particular technique that an actor can 'do', but a process: it can take place when any of Brecht's interpretative and performance approaches are employed.

Endnotes

1. 'From a Letter to an Actor', in *Brecht on Theatre*, ed. Marc Silberman, Steve Giles and Tom Kuhn (3rd Edition, London: Bloomsbury, 2015), p. 267.
2. *Ibid.*, p. 269.
3. Written in 1949, quoted in *ibid.*, p. 246.
4. Written in 1936–7, quoted in *ibid.*, p. 162.
5. Written in *c.* 1930, quoted in *ibid.*, p. 50.
6. Explained in John Rouse, 'Brecht and the Contradictory Actor', in Phillip B. Zarrilli, ed., *Acting (Re)Considered: A Theoretical and Practical Guide* (London: Routledge, 1995), p. 232.
7. See Brecht, Appendix to 'Short Description of a New Technique of Acting that Produces a *Verfremdung* Effect', and 'On Epic Dramatic Art', in *Brecht on Theatre*, ed. Silberman et al., pp. 192 and 197.
8. For the original phrases from which mine are derived, see Brecht, 'Old versus New Theatre', in *Brecht on Theatre*, ed. Silberman et al., pp. 111–12.
9. See Brecht, '*Messingkauf* or Buying Brass', in *Brecht on Performance: Messingkauf and Modelbooks*, ed. Tom Kuhn, Steve Giles and Marc Silberman (London: Bloomsbury, 2014), pp. 91–2.
10. *Brecht on Theatre*, ed. Silberman et al., p. 242.
11. See 'From a Letter to an Actor', in *ibid.*, pp. 267–70.
12. These ideas are discussed in immense detail in Brecht's 1941 essay 'On the Gradual Approach to the Study and Construction of the Figure', in *ibid.* pp. 198–200.
13. Anton Chekhov, *The Cherry Orchard* in *Chekhov: Four Plays*, translated by Stephen Mulrine (London: Nick Hern Books, 2005).
14. Maxim Gorky, *Philistines*, in a translation by Andrew Upton (London: Faber and Faber, 2007).
15. Brecht, 'A Short Organum for the Theatre', *Brecht on Theatre: The Development of an Aesthetic*, edited and translated by John Willett (New York: Hill and Wang, 1992), .p. 200.

16. *Brecht on Theatre*, ed. Silberman et al., p. 176.
17. Based on a real incident in 2015. See: https://www.cbsnews.com/news/mayor-southcarolina-police-officer-charged-with-murder-in-shooting-after-traffic-stop/
18. Bertolt Brecht, *Collected Plays: Eight*, ed. Tom Kuhn and David Constantine (London: Bloomsbury, 2015); see 'Phases of a Stage Direction', in *Brecht on Performance*, p. 230.
19. Carlos Murillo, *A Human Interest Story (or The Gory Details and All): A Play for Six Voices* (New York: Dramatists Play Service, 2009).
20. Declan Donnellan, *The Actor and The Target* (London: Nick Hern Books 2002), p. 80.
21. Harold Pinter, *Plays Two* (London: Faber and Faber, 1991), pp. 167–9.
22. David Mamet, *Oleanna* (London: Methuen, 1993), pp. 52–3.
23. David Hare, *Stuff Happens* (London: Faber and Faber, 2004), p. 45.
24. Chekhov, *Three Sisters*, in *Chekhov: Four Plays*, trans. Mulrine, pp. 174–6.
25. From 'A Short Organum for the Theatre', in *Brecht on Theatre: The Development of an Aesthetic*, ed. and trans. John Willett (London: Bloomsbury, 2013), p. 200.
26. Published in the essay 'Die *Antigone* des Sophokles: Material zur Antigone', quoted in translation in John Rouse, 'Brecht and The Contradictory Actor', *Theatre Journal* 36, No. 1 (1984).
27. Lee Strasberg, *At the Actors Studio: Tape-Recorded Sessions*, ed. Robert H. Hethmon (New York: Viking, 1965), p. 384.
28. A phrase frequently used by Brecht when discussing *Verfremdung*. It features heavily in 'Verfremdung Effects in Chinese Acting' (1936), in *Brecht on Theatre*, ed. Silberman et al, pp. 151–8.
29. See paragraph 58 of 'A Short Organon', in *Brecht on Theatre*, ed. Silberman et al., p. 247.
30. Keith Johnstone *Impro: Improvisation and the Theatre* (London: Methuen, 1981), p. 33.
31. From the essay 'More Good Sport' (1926), in *Brecht on Theatre*, ed. Silberman et al., p. 27.
32. This is how Brecht himself directed the peasant woman in scene 11 of *Mother Courage*, as she drops to her knees to pray that for the city of Halle. The meticulous and self-conscious performance of her prayer was a powerful expression of its futility.
33. This is based on an exercise introduced to me by David Shirley, Director of School of Theatre, Manchester Metropolitan University.
34. Hans Bunge, '*Der Kaukasische Kreidekreis*: Diary of a Production', Bertolt-Brecht-Archiv (945/100).
35. Included in a list of exercises immediately following the '*Street Scene*' essay in *Brecht on Theatre*, ed. and trans. John Willett, p. 129. (For some reason, this list was omitted from the 2015 third edition.)
36. *Ibid.*
37. Available online via the link: http://www.telegraph.co.uk/comment/3562917/Colonel-Tim-Collins-Iraq-war-speech-in-full.html

38. Available online via the link: https://www.youtube.com/watch?v=us3yqtCROt4.
39. BBC coverage of the event available online via the link: https://www.youtube.com/watch?v=0ZSzvuXMpoc (the ideal section begins at 3:32:36)
40. 'Schwierigkeiten des epischen Theaters', BFA 21/209-10, quoted in *Brecht on Theatre*, ed. Silberman et al., p. 39.
41. 'Appendix to the Short Organon for the Theatre', in *Brecht on Theatre*, ed. Silberman et al., p. 278.
42. *Ibid.*
43. Bertolt Brecht, *The Caucasian Chalk Circle*, translated by James and Tania Stern with W. H. Auden (London: Methuen, 1976), pp. 17–19.
44. 'From a Letter to an Actor' (1951), in *Brecht on Theatre*, ed. Silberman et al., p. 234.
45. *Brecht on Theatre*, ed. Silberman et al., p. 313.
46. Harold Pinter, *Celebration*, in *Plays: Four* (London: Faber and Faber, 2000), pp. 58–9.
47. *Brecht on Theatre*, ed. Silberman et al., pp. 198–200.
48. David Barnett, *Brecht in Practice: Theatre, Theory and Performance* (London: Bloomsbury, 2015), Chapter 6.
49. John Wright, *Why Is That So Funny? A Practical Exploration of Physical Comedy* (London: Nick Hern Books, 2015).
50. Walter Benjamin, *Understanding Brecht*, translated by Anna Bostock (London: Verso, 1998), p. 2.

Bibliography

Barnett, David, *Brecht in Practice: Theatre, Theory and Performance* (London: Bloomsbury, 2015)

Benjamin, Walter, *Understanding Brecht*, translated by Anna Bostock (London: Verso, 1998)

Brecht, Bertolt, *Brecht on Performance: Messingkauf and Modelbooks*, ed. Tom Kuhn, Steve Giles and Marc Silberman (London: Bloomsbury, London, 2015)

Brecht, Bertolt, *Brecht on Theatre*, ed. by Tom Kuhn, Steve Giles and Marc Silberman, 3rd edition (London: Bloomsbury, 2015)

Brecht, Bertolt, *Brecht on Theatre: The Development of an Aesthetic*, edited and translated by John Willett (New York: Hill and Wang, 1992; London: Methuen, 2013)

Donnellan, Declan, *The Actor and The Target* (London: Nick Hern Books, 2002; new edition 2005)

Johnstone, Keith, *Impro: Improvisation and the Theatre* (London: Methuen, 1981)

Mumford, Meg, *Bertolt Brecht*, Routledge Performance Practitioners (Oxford: Routledge, 2009)

Unwin, Stephen (with Julian Jones), *The Complete Brecht Toolkit* (London: Nick Hern Books, 2014)

Wright, Elizabeth, *Postmodern Brecht* (London: Routledge, 1989)

Wright, John, *Why Is That So Funny? A Practical Exploration of Physical Comedy* (London: Nick Hern Books, 2006)

Index

Index of Exercises

Alphabetical

www.nickhernbooks.co.uk